Flashes in the Darkness

THE FLASHLIGHT battery was wearing down, but the children's eyes had become accustomed to the darkness. Before them loomed two massive gray shapes with black wedges of the night sky cutting into them. In one of these wedges hung a star.

Suddenly there was a polar flash of white light, as if from that very star. The whisper in the wind became a cry, and a bleached shadow swirled up from the wedge between the rocks. It was as if a wisp of the Milky Way had torn loose from the sky.

> *I thought . . . I thought . . .* The whisper in the wind grew into a tremulous voice. *I thought you would never come!* And then laughter like wind chimes broke through the night. *But you have and I am so happy!*

The voice came to them through cosmic channels. July wondered if this were the cosmic background radiation that scientists pick up from deep space, a maverick radio wave. Whoever, knew better. This was the whisper carried on the wind that scraped the leaves against the screen of the bedroom window back in Washington, D.C. This was the whisper wrapped in the melody of the humpbacked flute player's song.

A Voice in the Wind

A Voice in the Wind

A STARBUCK TWINS MYSTERY, BOOK THREE

Kathryn Lasky

Harcourt, Inc.

ORLANDO AUSTIN NEW YORK SAN DIEGO LONDON

www.HarcourtBooks.com

Library of Congress Cataloging-in-Publication Data
Lasky, Kathryn.
A voice in the wind/Kathryn Lasky.
p.   cm.—(A Starbuck twins mystery; bk. 3)
Summary: The two sets of Starbuck twins, in New Mexico with
their father, meet a six-hundred-year-old Native American ghost and use
their telepathic powers to capture the looters of ancient Anasazi artifacts.
[1. Extrasensory perception—Fiction.   2. Twins—Fiction.   3. Brothers
and sisters—Fiction.   4. Ghosts—Fiction.   5. New Mexico—Fiction.
6. Indians of North America—Southwest, New—Fiction.   7. Mystery
and detective stories.]   I. Title.
PZ7.L3274Vo   2008
[Fic]—dc22   2007027500
ISBN 978-0-15-205875-3

Text set in Adobe Garamond
Designed by Cathy Riggs

A C E G H F D B

Printed in the United States of America

For Meribah, with love

1.

Vocabulary Tests
and Other Diseases
of the School Year

DIPHTHERIA—D-I-P-T-H-E-R—

No, July!

Liberty Starbuck mentally sent the message to her twin brother through the hallway that connected their turret bedrooms. Their rooms were on the third floor of their big old shingled house on shady tree-lined Dakota Street in Washington, D.C.

All four of the Starbuck children had amazing telepathic abilities. The younger set of twins, Charlotte and Amalie, nicknamed Charly and Molly, were six years old and identical. Liberty and July, born at midnight on the Fourth of July, were fraternal. But they were about as identical as a thirteen-year-old sister and brother could be, with their pale gray eyes, slashes of jet-black bangs, and the light bands of freckles that stretched across their noses. The strongest telepathic links existed within each set of twins. But when all four twins were together, they could cross-communicate and have entire conversations, which other people never heard, that they called teleflashing.

At this moment, Liberty was tuned in to July and was monumentally weary of his frustrating attempts to spell the word *diphtheria*. He could remember the definition: an acute contagious disease caused by infection with bacillus. But the spelling got him worse than the disease ever would!

Look, July, it's got this rhythm to it: di-ph-th-er-ia. You just have to get the pattern: da-duh-da-duh-da-duh-da-duh-da-duh. The beat tripped through the telepathic channels and met a dead end, followed by a groan.

Within seconds, Liberty and July were out from behind their desks; they nearly collided in Liberty's doorway.

"I can't believe this!" July was muttering out loud. "This is our first test in years!"

"It seems like forever since we've been stuck in regular school." Liberty sighed, flopping onto her bed. "First London, then Florida . . . Something always comes up."

"Charly and Molly are already being assigned reading groups. They've got their phonics workbooks," July said ominously.

As if on cue, the red-haired twins appeared at the doorway. Charly and Molly were mirror-image twins, as biologically identical as any twins could be. The only noticeable differences between them were their cowlicks and their birthmarks. Charly's cowlick swirled to the right; Molly's swirled left. And while Molly had a faint strawberry-colored birthmark on her right ear, Charly's appeared on her left ear. They truly were mirror images of each other. The twins were sometimes a shock to the unaccustomed eye. Their blazing red hair stood out in defiant little spikes all over their heads—except when they were wearing their Davy Crockett coonskin caps, a present from Grandma Starbuck. Due to their habit of sucking on the coons' tails, there were usually a few wisps of coon fur mingled in with the glaze that constantly glistened between the twins' noses and upper lips. On any given day, at least eleven of their combined twenty fingers wore press-on nails. Sometimes the nails had fancy designs, such as polka dots or lightning bolts, but today the twins had toned it down—bloodred dagger tips clutched the workbooks in their hands. The smell of wet fur and hair mousse—Charly and Molly loved hair mousse—surrounded them. Add to this a dash of the salty smell of perspiration. Liberty looked at her little sisters and wrinkled her nose. Unbelievable! How could any two people who had started out so cute have become so totally revolting? Waves of their signature fragrance—mousse, kid sweat, and fur—swirled through the air.

Charly and Molly looked absolutely miserable. Their immense blue eyes were swimming with sadness.

"We don't know how to read anymore," Charly wailed.

"It doesn't work," Molly whimpered.

"What are you two talking about?" July said. "What do you mean you don't know how anymore?"

"You can't forget it. It's like swimming," Liberty said.

"Or riding a bike," July added. "Just a few days ago you were reading everything."

"We can't read *their* way," Molly hissed defiantly.

Charly leaned forward, pressing her face close to Liberty's. She lowered her voice as if sharing a horrible revelation. "We can't read because we don't know the sound of silent *e*."

July and Liberty looked blankly at each other.

How the heck do you explain silent e?

Everybody knows this dumb silent e *sound except us. We feel left out.* Molly's whining drizzled into the channels like mist that was almost rain.

Left and *out* in combination were the two ugliest words in the English language, as far as Charly and Molly were concerned. July and Liberty knew that all too well.

They feel left out? Liberty was perplexed.

Left out of what?

Reading, you numbskull, Molly flared telepathically at her brother.

Oh, gosh. They're thinking of it like some secret code, Liberty moaned. *It's not like that at all, really. Silent* e *doesn't have a sound. That's the whole point.*

We don't get it, Molly and Charly flashed in unison.

What's there to get? July asked.

J. B., there's a lot to get. They used to know how to read. July's nickname was J. B., which was short for Jelly Bean, which stood for July Burton, his whole legal name.

Look. Silent e, Liberty explained, *doesn't have a sound of its own. It just changes how you say other sounds.* The little twins looked mystified.

Don't try to explain, Liberty. They were reading fine before they thought it was all so fancy and had this . . . this system.

Secret system, Molly added, narrowing her eyes as she contemplated the great conspiracy against her and her twin sister.

You see, that's just the problem with school. They make everything seem harder than it is, much more complicated, and then you get these two little guys who were doing just fine with Zanny, and now . . . July had practically succeeded in bringing tears to all of their eyes. He and Liberty thought that Charly and Molly seemed almost appealingly vulnerable despite their daggerlike nails and smeary noses.

Zanny Duggan was their all-time favorite babysitter. And when the Starbuck twins went along on business trips with their father, Putnam, Zanny became Zanny the Nanny, teacher as well as babysitter. Madeline Starbuck, the children's mother, owned and operated the largest tutu factory in the United States—Starbuck Recital Wear—and could not spend extended periods of time away from the business. She joined the rest of the family for a week or so each month when they were away. But someone had to be there on the spot for the four youngsters, and Zanny was everyone's first choice. Since she was a teacher, too, and made learning about a thousand times more interesting than it usually was in school, the Starbuck children had simply not gone to school recently. And Zanny had seen to it that they were way ahead in every subject.

Now it was back to vocabulary tests and phonics workbooks. What had happened to real books with real stories? And who gave a hoot whether you could spell diphtheria or not? Wasn't the point not to get the awful disease? What had happened to life? To adventure? To excitement?

What would Zanny do in this situation? July flashed.

I know exactly what she would do. Charly, Molly, and July looked at Liberty expectantly. *She would say to forget this silent* e *stuff, to read something that interests you and show the teacher what you can do. Once they see how well Charly and Molly read, they'll forget all about this phonics stuff.*

Really? the little twins asked.

Of course, Liberty flashed. *You little guys are really smart. You've always known what to do with silent* e.

Liberty's right. You guys have never met a silent e *you couldn't handle.*

Gee, we haven't? Charly and Molly seemed almost disappointed that the big secret was actually no secret at all.

No, you haven't. Tomorrow just go and show them your stuff.

"Now you guys should go to bed," Liberty said out loud. She could hear the approaching footsteps of their father.

"No, no, not time for bed." Putnam poked his shiny bald head into the room. He was smiling broadly. "Wait till you see the extension I've built for Home Run. It now reaches to the bottom of the stairs, all the way into the front entrance hall!"

Oh my gosh! Liberty and July flashed in sync.

Molly and Charly had bought Home Run, their pet hamster, a few weeks before. Since then, Putt had devoted himself, and all of the plastic soda bottles he could scrounge, to designing and building the world's most fabulous rodent environment. Using plastic bottles and PVC piping, Putt had built the hamster a runway that went from the attic into the little twins' room and then downstairs, for a grand total of an eighth of a mile of linear running, playing, exercising, and meditating space for Home Run. Home Run also had a clear plastic ball that he could travel about the house in.

This man needs a job, Liberty flashed.

He has a job, Liberty. He is just temporarily unoccupied.

Putnam Starbuck did have a very important job, with the Environmental Protection Agency. He traveled all over, helping catch toxic-waste crooks and doing surveys about how to best clean up messes and save endangered species. But a snag in the preparations for his next assignment meant that, for the time being, Putnam was stuck at home in Washington, D.C., doing anything he could think of to keep busy. One more week like this and Home Run's rodent runway would probably be creeping out of the brown shingled house on Dakota Street and up Pennsylvania Avenue to the White House.

"I just have one question." Madeline Starbuck stood in the doorway. "With an eighth of a mile of runway, most of which is PVC piping that you cannot see through, why, oh why, does Home Run elect to make his bathroom in the transparent part?"

The jingling sound of the hamster's rolling plastic ball passed by the doorway.

"Is the baby gate up?" everyone screamed, and they rushed out of the room. Charly dived and tackled the clear plastic ball just before it could roll off the top step and bounce, with Home Run in it, down the twenty-three hardwood steps to the landing below.

"Phew!" the Starbucks gasped in relief.

"I think I might build a little track for the ball to roll in." Putt scratched his chin. "You see, if it were on a track, you know, like one of those grooves for returning bowling balls, then . . ."

"Putt." Madeline's brow crinkled with concern. "Any word on the New Mexico project?"

Putt shook his head. "Still some politics going on. Things have to get ironed out first, and there's no telling how long that'll take."

Liberty and July felt a twinge as they envisioned the unfurling of endless weeks of vocabulary tests and book reports, and hours spent in classrooms.

"Time to go to bed," Madeline said. "Come on, kids. This is a school night, you know."

We know too well, July teleflashed.

Something's bound to happen, J. B. Something always does, Liberty answered bravely. But there was a quavering pulse in the teleflash, and it seemed to J. B. as if Liberty was hoping for a sign that something really would happen.

That night, as Liberty lay in bed, she heard the trees rustling outside her window. The turning leaves scraped against the shingles of the turret bedrooms and the eaves of the roof. It was a cool autumn wind from the west. It smelled different from the heavy summer breezes that swirled with the scent of the slow-moving, muddy river, of the sweet perfumy flowers that mixed in with the city fumes of buses and cars.

Liberty was teetering on that milky edge between waking and dreaming when a sudden gust struck the half-open window. There was a raspy, almost human sound. Liberty jerked awake, startled. It was just leaves—just leaves, she told herself. And, indeed, pressed against the screen were the slender leaves of the elm tree. As the wind died, the leaves fell on the sill, pale yellow, with barely a trace of their summer green. Yet there had been another sound embedded in the rustling. It was more like a whisper—like a muffled voice in the wind.

2.

Aunt Honey's Big Idea

"I DON'T KNOW whether to laugh or cry," Madeline said to Putt before dinner the next day. She looked up as Liberty and July came through the door into the living room, then ran her fingers through the gray-flecked hair that framed her face, and bit her lip, puzzled. Putt appeared somewhat bewildered as well. Madeline held an orchid-colored piece of fancy writing paper in one hand.

A communiqué from the Great One, Liberty teleflashed.

Old Honey Buns herself! July exclaimed. *Who else has that disgusting color for writing paper?*

Her signature color, she calls it.

Aunt Honey was clearly not the twins' favorite relative. She meant well, but she was bossy and interfering. Although she and Madeline were twins, they were definitely not identical.

"Cry," Liberty said to her mother as she stared at the orchid-colored piece of paper. "Definitely cry. How could you think about laughing? This is no laughing matter. This is Aunt Honey."

July took the letter and began to read it aloud.

"'Dearest Madeline and Putt, and my four little delectable nieces and nephew—'"

Could you barf? Liberty flashed. *She always compares us to food.*

Be glad she doesn't call you a brussels sprout, what with her being a vegetarian. Now shut up and let me read this.

"'I am so excited about the possibility of your coming out here to New Mexico.' Aunt Honey is in New Mexico?"

"Yes, remember, dear?" Madeline replied. "She went to visit an old friend of hers who owns a health and beauty spa."

"It was supposed to be just a visit," Liberty said ominously. "Read on."

"'You will love it here. And now for the really great news. I have had such a marvelous time at Roz's spa, Rancho Eleganza, and you know they have this wonderful ice-skating rink. I have been giving demos and lessons. There are an amazing number of ladies here who remember me from my old Ice Capers days—well, guess what?'" In an apprehensive whisper, July continued. "'Roz would like me to stay on and teach ice-skating as part of the health and beauty program through the winter. Isn't that grand, especially if it all works out for you to come out here, too? One big happy family in the high-desert country.'"

I think I'm going to be sick, July flashed.

Putnam sighed. "Well, I did get another letter today. But seeing as I am a sensitive sort of father"—he paused—"and knowing how you feel about your aunt Honey, I don't know if you will greet this as good news or bad news. You see, my assignment in New Mexico has been confirmed."

July blinked. "Does this mean that—"

Madeline raised a hand. "Don't worry. I've already called Zanny. We'll leave for New Mexico next week."

July, anything that causes us to miss the vocabulary test is worth it! Liberty flashed.

The blue-striped pepper fish had been the reason for the delay in Putnam's assignment from the Environmental Protection Agency. For months a battle had raged between certain environmentalists and the Native Americans in the region of the Spirit River. What was more important, July and Liberty had heard Putt fume to his wife, that a rare and endangered fish be preserved or that people who were living in terrible poverty be allowed to have a chance to farm, and improve their economic condition? The diversion of the river could provide success for one species—humans—and doom for another, the blue-striped pepper fish. Diversion of rivers often altered the conditions to which fish were accustomed. The Environmental Protection Agency and most scientists agreed that in this case, the economic improvement of the impoverished Native Americans was more important than the blue-striped pepper fish. Furthermore, it was doubtful that the fish would be harmed at all, for they did not live in this river itself, but in a tributary. It had been a tough decision, but one with which Putnam had agreed. Although continuing protests from a small group of environmentalists had delayed the project, now the delays were over, the snags untangled, and the hitches unhitched. Except for one: Aunt Honey and her ice-skating rink.

"How far away will Aunt Honey be, anyway?" Molly asked.

"Fifteen or twenty miles or so," Madeline said. That seemed pretty far away to the children.

"Of course," added Putt, "distances out there in the wide-open spaces are nothing. Twenty miles—it's like just around the block here."

What's really worse, July thought as he lay in bed that night, diphtheria or Aunt Honey?

Oh, come on now, July! Aren't you being a tad dramatic? Liberty flashed from her bedroom, where she was sitting by her open window, her elbows resting on the sill.

Let me rephrase the question: Is it worse having to spell diphtheria *on a school test or having Aunt Honey a block away?*

It's not a block. Twenty miles is still twenty miles. She's not going to want to come over to what's-it-called.

Tres Arroyos.

Yeah, that's it. No way is she going to leave all that health and beauty spa stuff—mud baths, ice-skating, massages. I know our aunt Honey.

Some leaves scuttled against the bottom of the window screen. Liberty raised the screen a few inches and reached for them. They felt like dry husks, crisp and lifeless. But a west wind had whistled through them the night before just as she had been falling asleep. She could have sworn then that she had heard a voice in that wind—smothered, yet with a human clarity. Liberty looked now at the curling leaves in her hand. "Silly!" she muttered and walked back to her bed. She put the leaves on her bedside table and crawled under the covers.

Long after everyone was asleep, the curtains on the turret window billowed with wind. The leaves on the bedside table swirled up in the sudden gust and floated down onto Liberty's pillow. She was sleeping so deeply that the voice that came on the wind did not even startle her. It was an ancient voice, yet somehow young, melting out of a far time. Liberty struggled through the fog of sleep to hear the voice. Just one word, she thought in her sleep, just one word. *Ott . . . ott?* No, something was missing. She pressed through the misty vapors further. *Ott . . . Po . . . ottt . . . Pot! Cue me, co-me? Come pot?* Liberty turned and sighed. The voice whispered. She turned again. July, too, yawned and turned over, as if sensing the voice lacing through his sister's dreams.

But in the morning, the children remembered nothing—not a voice, not a whisper, not a wind. Liberty picked the leaves up off the floor by her bed and put them in her wastebasket.

3.

Land of Clear Light
and Purple Shadows

THE CLOUD cover had begun to thin, almost imperceptibly at first, but gradually the clearing became more noticeable. The faint haze that had covered the land below the plane like a fuzzy mohair blanket soon blew away entirely.

"The Pacific westerlies," Putt said, turning around in the seat he occupied next to Madeline and in front of Liberty, July, and Zanny. "We're flying out of the wet air of the Texas Panhandle, the air that comes up from the Gulf of Mexico, and into the mountain and desert air. It's dry— dried by hundreds of mountain ranges and miles and miles of desert in between. The westerlies make everything very clear."

Liberty pressed her cheek against the window and looked down. Under the wing tip, the tan, featureless land stretched out endlessly. As she pulled her thoughts away from the view outside the plane window, she became aware of a soft giggle rippling from the front of the airplane. Then she heard Zanny's shocked voice. "Oh, no!"

It was Home Run, rolling down the aisle in his plastic ball. He was supposed to have been checked into Sky Cuddle, the air pet-care service. But in the confusion of checking baggage, everyone had forgotten, and the little twins had carried Home Run and his plastic ball aboard in Aunt Honey's old bowling ball case. They usually packed their makeup in it.

"Just a minute, I'll catch him." Charly's voice rang out, and the passengers burst into laughter as the little girl ran down the aisle after the ball with the furry critter inside. A businessman reached out from his aisle seat and stopped Home Run. A flight attendant, looking slightly dazed, stopped in her tracks and stared down in disbelief. "It's a hamster!" she whispered.

"Phew." Charly wiped her brow. "Don't worry," she reassured the flight attendant. "He's very friendly, and he only pees in his plastic ball here."

Then Molly appeared in the aisle to assist Charly, and soon nearly everyone on the plane was cooing over the peculiar little twosome and their pet in the plastic ball.

"Look at them—aren't they adorable!"

"Most identical twins I ever saw!"

"Mirror-image identical," Charly said.

"Yep," confirmed Molly, taking off her coonskin cap. "See our cowlicks?" Charly handed Home Run to the flight attendant who was pushing the drink cart and took off her own cap, too. Soon they were giving the surrounding passengers a lecture on the meaning and intricacies of mirror-image identical twins. They showed them their clockwise and counterclockwise cowlicks, as well as their birthmarks. Then they stood opposite each other so the passengers could get the full effect of the mirror image. "Dr. Goldspoon, our pediatrician, says we are the most identical twins he has ever seen," Charly told the attentive passengers.

"Well, mercy me!" said an older lady as she touched Molly's cheek lightly and studied her face. "It seems like a miracle." Molly and Charly beamed angelically.

Is this enough to make you throw up? Liberty flashed.

Shut up. They think we're cute, flashed Molly.

Yeah, pointy noses! added Charly.

Listen, our noses might be pointy, but at least they're not gushing slime like yours, July flashed.

At that, both little twins simultaneously raised their arms, Charly her left and Molly her right, and wiped their noses. The passengers went into absolute ecstasy. They had never in their lives seen anything so adorable.

Oh, pass me the airsick bag, Liberty telesquealed.

Oh, lord, get this, July flashed.

"Well, it's not really a miracle that we're this way. There is a scientific explanation," Charly was saying authoritatively. The audience tensed in anticipation.

"You see," Molly continued, "with mirror-image identical twins the fertilized egg splits between the tenth and the thirteenth day after . . ."

Good grief, I don't believe this—a midair sex lecture!
This is the most embarrassing moment of my life!

"Mom! Do something!" Liberty hissed.

Putt did do something, and he did stop Charly and Molly from continuing their sex lecture. But as soon as the words were out of his mouth, he knew what he said was wrong. "This is very embarrassing for your brother and sister."

Then every head in the plane, it seemed to Liberty and July, turned around and looked at them.

"Why, look, another set!"

"My heavens, they look identical, too."

"No," piped up Molly. "One's a boy and one's a girl, but Dr. Goldspoon says they're the most identical fraternal twins that he's ever seen, but when they undress . . ."

I don't believe this! Liberty telescreamed.

"Coffee, tea, soft drinks, juice?" the flight attendant asked Zanny.

"How about a parachute?" July muttered.

Within minutes of driving out of the airport in Albuquerque in their rental Rough Rider van, the Starbucks and Zanny were heading west under a flawless turquoise sky.

Signs of civilization became fewer and farther between—an occasional billboard, a convenience store, a gas station. The land flattened and the road grew bumpier. They hopscotched through the reservation land—some Navajo, some Pueblo. They sliced through a corner of the Acoma and the Zuni Indians' country and then, for a stretch, were on federally owned land. Familiar types of stores gave way to trading posts, where local Indians sold woven rugs, silver concha belts, turquoise jewelry, and pottery and bought everything from food and tires to tools and seed. It was hard to imagine growing things here, July thought as he looked out the window. The land was dry and harsh, yet mysteriously beautiful.

As the light fell across the country, the mountains appeared sharp against the sky. The light kept changing. The mountains, buff-colored minutes before, began to turn a dusky mauve. The van wound through canyons dotted with piñon trees, then up again to higher land where strange rock formations writhed out of the ground like fantastic beasts. Occasional road signs indicated a creek or a "wash," which Putnam explained was a dried-up streambed. In this empty land that seemed to have no boundaries, the natural features became the reference points and the names for places. There was a Chaco Wash and a Tsaya Wash and a Red Wash, and places with strange-sounding names like Tsoodzil that linked the land to the oldest cultures in the New World.

Zanny had told the children that "New World" was a white man's name for a very old place. This world had been here long, long before the Spanish and the Europeans came to explore it.

"A hogan!" Putnam exclaimed. "Our first hogan! We're in Navajo country for sure." He slowed the van down and pointed out the window. The land fell away into a shallow basin. A dirt road wound off toward a cluster of rocks that popped out of the ground like giant elephant legs and cast long shadows in the afternoon light. Where the shadows ended was a dome-shaped cabin made of logs. Putnam pulled the car to the side of the road so they could have a better look.

"See, it's an octagon, eight sides," Putnam said. "There's the smoke hole in the center. No smoke, though. Nobody home, I guess."

"Do the Indians live in them?" Liberty asked.

"Yes, they certainly do."

They drove on. More rocks, with flat tablelike surfaces on top, climbed out of the broken land.

"We're getting closer to Tres Arroyos. You can tell by all these mesas," Putt said.

"What are mesas?" Charly asked.

"These land formations." Putt pointed out the window. "They look like big flat tabletops lifting high up from the ground. Some of them are so big that whole villages have been built on top of them. Many Navajos live in hogans; some still herd sheep in the lonely stretches of high-desert country. Pueblos live in rock and adobe villages, often tending communally owned fields."

Suddenly Putnam swerved the van sharply onto the shoulder of the road.

"What in the world!" shrieked Madeline.

"A ruin! Right on schedule."

"Ruin? You nearly wrecked the car and ruined your family!" Madeline was irritated.

"Oh!" gasped Liberty. In front of them was an expanse of rugged broken land that ended at a red rock cliff face. Under its overhang a jumble of large cubes seemed to hang in midair, their many levels connected by terraces.

"It's an Anasazi cliff dwelling!" Zanny's voice swelled with delight. She rolled down the window and stuck her head out. "A genuine ruin and a lovely one at that."

They drove closer and got out of the car to get a better look. Compared to the scale of the cliff and the immense arch of the sky, the pueblo looked like a miniature village constructed from children's building blocks. The simple geometric shapes were arranged in a pleasing pattern of terraces that followed the contours of the land and the mountains.

"Can we go explore?" Liberty asked. Then all the twins began clamoring, "Please! Please! We want to explore."

"Oh, dear, it's getting late . . . ," Madeline said.

"Yes, it is turning chilly . . . and we do have more driving to do," Putt added.

Charly said the deciding words. "It's educational!"

"Part of the Southwest curriculum," the four twins said at once, and looked at Zanny.

On all their adventures, Zanny dreamed up special courses to fit the particular place the Starbucks were living. This time it would be the Southwest curriculum, with the focus on the Native Americans of the Four Corners area, the region where the corners of New Mexico, Colorado, Utah, and Arizona came together. This was the land where the Pueblos and the Navajo still lived, where the Anasazi, known as "The Ancient Ones," had lived and then mysteriously vanished almost two hundred years before Columbus arrived in the West Indies.

All eyes were turned toward Zanny. Zanny looked at Madeline, Madeline looked at Putt, and they all got out of the van and started walking toward the ruin. They walked in a loose line over broken ground, which was dotted with silvery green sagebrush and spires of bristling cactus, toward the cliff that seemed to change color in the setting sun. The rock turned from soft red to rose to deep amber and finally to dusky purple.

The family stood in the lavender shadows of the overhanging cliff. They had climbed up onto a terrace, and although they were cold, not one twin dared show it. It was a strange place, this ruin. The small windows pierced in the two-foot-thick adobe walls seemed like ghost eyes from a time long, long ago. What had the ghost eyes seen?

Children playing on these terraces?

What a neat place to live!

So high up.

You could reach out your window and touch a cloud.

It's like a city in the sky!

The telepathic channels were busy as the children tried to imagine how people had lived in this odd place.

"Look over there, kids," Zanny said, pointing to a high rock wall about twenty feet up. "Do you see those pictures on the rock? They're called petroglyphs."

"Oh, yeah!" July said softly.

Almost straight above them, carved into the rock, was a series of shapes, some simple geometric ones, others the contours of animals.

"I see a frog!" Molly exclaimed.

"I think I see a snake," Liberty said.

"And look at the men with bird feet sort of hopping around," July said.

"Does anyone see a flute player?" Zanny asked.

"Flute player?" they all said.

"Yes, a humpbacked figure playing a flute. He was a favorite spirit of the Anasazi—a kind of god. They called him Kokopelli."

"What do all these pictures mean?" July asked, scrunching up his face to better see them and to try and read their meaning. But the ancient code seemed to escape all the children.

"This is worse than silent *e*," Molly muttered.

"They're like messages from the past, before we could read—any of us," July said.

"Maybe they're like little stone prayers," Liberty whispered.

"Zanny." July, his head tilted back, slowly surveyed the rock face. "How would they get from here to up there to carve those pictures or even get to other houses that were higher or lower down? There aren't any stairs."

"They used ladders a lot. They're called kiva ladders because they were used to go down into the kivas, which are the chambers where they had their religious ceremonies. But they used the ladders for other places, too, and would prop them up against the walls and just go climbing to visit a neighbor."

"Just go climbing." Liberty's voice was soft. The lives behind these pictures seemed too distant to imagine. She was sad that she could not picture these people better. It was a beautiful place, but it was still just a ruin. And if people had really lived here, where had they all gone? That was what Zanny had said was the biggest mystery of all. Why had the Anasazi left their beautiful villages, suspended in the air? Why had they vanished, leaving no clue as to what had driven them from their cliff dwellings in the turquoise sky? Liberty looked out across the desert country. Elongated purple clouds swam low through the sky like pods of sleek whales. Below the clouds, the sun had just slipped away over the horizon. A soft glow from the last rays lingered, a memory of the day's light, hanging like a veil between twilight and total darkness. And standing, faceless and forgotten behind the veil, were the people, the Ancient Ones, forever lost. Liberty wanted so badly just to believe that they had been here once—once upon a real time. She wanted to see their faces. A chill wind blew a strand of her hair across her cheek.

"Come on, Liberty!" She heard her mom call. The rest of the family had already started to walk toward the van. Liberty scrambled down from the terrace and caught up with them. They were on their way to their new home in the high desert.

4.

The House on the Mesa

"THIS IS SO neat!" July exclaimed.

"The government is really paying for this?" Liberty asked.

"I sure hope so," Madeline said as she looked at the large adobe house. Although the house was big, it appeared snug, pressed between the dark sky and the mesa on which it perched. It seemed to grow straight out of the gingerbread-colored rock; its shape fit the contours of the land. It was hard to imagine that hammer and nails or bulldozers and shovels had been a part of the construction of this house. And the ladders that had been missing at the cliff dwellings were here, waiting to be climbed.

Putt and Madeline entered through the front door, but Zanny could not resist following the kids, who were scrambling up and down ladders from one terrace to another and climbing through the windows and skylights that popped up through several parts of the roof. Their new home felt like a treehouse made of rock and adobe.

"Let me up! Let me up! Get out of the way." Liberty clambered up the ladder behind July in the bedroom they would share. The ladder poked up through a skylight between the immense ceiling beams, and when July slid open the skylight, a cascade of vines with tiny yellow blossoms the size of parakeets' feet fell through the opening. July climbed through, and Liberty quickly followed.

"It's a whole garden on the roof. Can you believe it!" July exclaimed.

But what Liberty could not believe as she climbed up and flung back her head was the garden of stars in the sky. In the black velvet night, the stars seemed close enough to reach out and touch. A flood of silver moonlight illuminated the distant cliffs.

There was a clarity to the night that neither July nor Liberty had ever seen. The house on the mesa was so far away from the glow of any city or the smoky fumes of any machines that the sky seemed to become part of the earth and the earth part of the sky. The two worlds, once separate, were one.

In the distance, they heard a long, low howl.

"What's that?" Liberty whispered.

"A coyote, I bet," July said.

Liberty hunched her shoulders against the cold and shivered. She felt her shoulder blades move and for a brief moment wondered whether those bones, the ones her mom called angel wings, had magically sprouted into real wings and brought her close to heaven.

The twins climbed back down the ladder into the bedroom. They had never slept in a room quite like this one. There was a fireplace that emerged from the wall as if it had grown there. Instead of regular beds, there were *bancos,* or adobe benches, which seemed to sprout right out of the walls. The mattresses were covered with beautiful, handwoven, wide-striped blankets in bright reds and oranges. Deep niches had been carved in the walls above the *bancos;* there July and Liberty could keep books or a clock or just about anything. In one niche, they put a tin box of jelly beans, July's bust of Sherlock Holmes, a magnifying glass, and a pipe— Sherlock Holmes was one of their favorites.

I like this place, Liberty thought as she climbed under her heavy striped blanket.

Me, too, flashed July, picking up on her thoughts.

Madeline walked in carrying some small logs under one arm and a book under the other.

"It gets cold here at night. I'm going to teach you how to build a fire. I think I still remember from my old Girl Scout days. Although this will be a little different because it's not exactly a campfire." She sat back on her heels and studied the oddly shaped fireplace. It was very deep and conical. Liberty and July hopped out of bed.

"The same principles must apply," Madeline said as she put down the logs. "But it won't work to lay the logs down flat on their sides. You prop them up on their ends instead." She demonstrated, then said, "Here, you do it, kids." Liberty and July propped the logs into a tent shape.

"Good. Now stick in some paper and some kindling." Madeline pointed at a small pine chest against the wall.

Within minutes a fire was crackling in the fireplace. The propped-up logs looked like a flaming tepee and threw off a good amount of heat.

"What's that book, Mom?" Liberty asked.

"A story I was reading to Charly and Molly about how the Navajo thought the world was created. It's kind of interesting. It's mostly about animals—very smart animals—but the book calls them people. There were the Air Spirit People."

"The Air Spirit People?" Liberty remembered how she had stood on the rooftop, where the separation between earth and sky had melted away, where she could almost reach out and touch a star. She had felt the wind in her hair and had indeed felt like some sort of air spirit.

"Would you read us a little bit of the story?" July asked, as he and Liberty crawled back into their beds.

"Sure." Madeline sat down in a pine chair by the fireplace, spread an Indian blanket across her knees, and began to read.

"'In the beginning, when the world was new and all the people and the animals were the same and spoke the same language, not even the insects had wings . . .'"

Madeline read the story of how the Air Spirit People of the first small, dark place left that world behind. They crawled out of the black world and, with the help of Dragonfly, found a brighter, wider world.

"'"Where will we go?" asked the ants,'" Madeline read. She squeezed her normally husky voice into a smaller ant-sized one. "'Dragonfly answered, "We must go to some other land. To do that, we need wings."

"'"Wings?" said the ants, for none of these insects knew about wings. But Dragonfly was smart and inventive, and even though she had never seen wings, she knew that wings were what was needed.'" Madeline said, "I think you call that intuition."

"Keep reading," July said.

"'So,'" continued Madeline, "'Dragonfly made herself a double set of wings with thin, transparent chips of mica and flew up to the top of the black dome of the sky to look for a crack. Others began building wings for themselves, too. It was Locust who spotted the faint blue light shining through a crack in the ceiling of the black sky.'"

Madeline told how the animals passed into the next world—the Blue World with the arching blue sky. After a while, the voice of the Blue Wind called, beckoning the insects to yet another world, the Yellow World. All was well in the Yellow World for a long time, until it became too crowded and "neighbor fought neighbor." The pack rat stole from the bear and the chipmunk stole from the ground squirrel and the coyote stole from everyone. In fact, Coyote was the one who had taught all the other animals how to steal. And he was the best at it.

The children were growing sleepy but they begged Madeline to keep reading.

"I only got to the second world with Charly and Molly," she said.

"How many more worlds are there?" Liberty asked sleepily.

"Two."

"Keep reading."

Liberty and July fell asleep somewhere between the fourth and the fifth worlds. They were never quite sure which parts they dreamed and which parts Madeline read. But there was a flood before the fourth world, and there was a hollow reed. It was through the reed that the creatures escaped to the fifth world, on the earth's surface. Liberty remembered something about Spider weaving a ladder and hooking it onto Dragonfly, who had flown into the next sky and looped herself into a hook.

By the time Madeline climbed up the ladder to close the skylight partway, the children were fast asleep. She kissed her older twins good night and touched them lightly on their backs where angel wings might grow. She would be here for only a few days this time, helping the family to settle in before she flew back to Washington for the fall sales conference and a series of meetings. She must try to get out more than once a month, Madeline thought. This assignment of Putt's was his most difficult yet, and he would be more distracted than usual. Zanny was wonderful, but she couldn't do everything. And how lovely it had been reading to the older twins again. She turned and walked out under the swooping pine limb that formed the top of the door frame, then looked up at it and smiled. What a perfect house this was for them—no harsh angles, just higgledy-piggledy lines, the perfect contours for a higgledy-piggledy family that never quite followed the rules.

Everyone in the house on the mesa had been sleeping deeply for hours when the wind stirred a few of the vines that fell through the skylight in Liberty and July's room. The little blossoms printed a pattern on the moon-washed adobe wall. Liberty sighed, turned over on her back, and pulled the blanket up to her chin. A few embers still glowed in the fireplace. She opened her eyes and peered through the skylight. Was she dreaming or was she awake? Was that the faithful dragonfly twinkling above her in the night, and were these vines the spider's ladder that reached into a new world? She turned over and drifted into a kaleidoscopic dream of parakeets' feet and spiderwebs, of stone wings and crafty coyotes. And through the dream there blew a wind, and within the wind there was a voice. No longer smothered, the voice was clear but distant, as if it were calling from a deep, deep canyon.

5.

Honey Buns and Tortillas

"I'M HERE!" a voice trilled. There was a tapping on the windowpane. Liberty heard her brother moan slightly, then say, "Good grief, I don't believe it!"

"What?" Liberty rolled over sleepily and looked. She rubbed her eyes, rubbed them again, and thought twice about speaking out loud.

Oh no! she flashed.

Oh yes! July responded.

It's not a dream.

Not a dream, Liberty.

Well, I guess you can't call it a nightmare. How the heck did she get up here?

The ladders, remember?

Peering through the window was none other than Aunt Honey in an immense white cowboy hat with a turquoise-

and-silver band around its rim. Her head filled the window, blotting out a distant mountain, the sky, and the sun.

"May I come in?" she inquired cheerfully and raised the window, which had been left open a few inches to let in the night air. "I've already gone in through the door. Your mom showed me which window was yours. Isn't this ladder stuff a hoot?"

Well, just hoot on, Honey, July telemuttered. *I cannot stand people who are this perky in the morning!*

Come on, J. B., we gotta be nice.

Just remember that Aunt Honey is very well meaning, as Mom says. Liberty periodically adopted this mature attitude. It was her way of saying that the four-minute head start July got at birth didn't count for much. Aunt Honey was, in fact, the ultimate challenge to one's maturity. She was the litmus test for patience and fair play.

"Come on in, Aunt Honey."

Good grief, you sound as perky as she does! I think I'm going to be sick. July sank back into the pillows.

There was a sudden total eclipse as Aunt Honey's backside reared through the window frame. As she swung a leg and then the rest of her body through the opening, there was a tiny ripping noise.

"Uh-oh! My jeans . . . And I have lost weight at the spa—five pounds. This must be stressing them."

Stressing them! July flashed.

Shut up, J. B. You're so immature sometimes. I think it's nice and really cute the way she climbed up here just to say good morning.

"Good morning, children! Oh, isn't this divine? I think it's just marvelous that you are living in such an authentic dwelling." She clapped her hands and did a little spin, as if she were still on her old Ice Capers skates.

"What an experience!"

Aunt Honey was large, though not really fat, and it was hard to take her in at a single glance, especially in this outfit. But Liberty spotted a little glittering gold pin on Aunt Honey's vest.

"What's that pin you're wearing, Aunt Honey?" she asked.

Honey looked down at her vest. "My coyote pin. It's kind of like the symbol of Rancho Eleganza, the spa. They have it on all their towels and bathrobes, and you can buy these pins in the gift shop. Not real diamonds in the eyes, of course, but still quite lovely."

"Why a coyote?"

"Why not? The coyote, you know, is one of the most delightful characters in Indian folklore. A kind of funny little fellow, a jolly trickster, always up for a good laugh or a prank. At Rancho Eleganza we try to emphasize the positive and not take ourselves too seriously, you know."

Is that why she's teaching ice-skating in the desert to fat ladies? July flashed.

Just then Charly and Molly dropped through the skylight.

"Why you guys sleepin' so late?" Molly said, scrambling down the ladder and taking a flying leap onto July's bed.

"Is there no peace around here? Is there no privacy?" July roared.

"Are you in a bad mood or something, July?" Molly asked.

"How'd you guess?" Liberty muttered.

"Did he get up on the wrong side of the bed?" Charly laughed. "Get the joke?" In case anyone had missed it, she added, "There's only one side to these beds that you can get out of." She dissolved into giggles.

"Children, why don't we get out of here and let July and Liberty get up on their own. We'll see you two at breakfast in a few minutes," Aunt Honey said.

"Definitely." Liberty could smell sausage cooking downstairs and she just bet her mother was making pancakes. She was pretty hungry, and she wasn't going to wait around for July, who was watching Aunt Honey try to climb back out the window. Molly and Charly had already gone up the ladder, through the skylight, and down yet another ladder to their own bedroom on a lower level. Nobody seemed the least bit attracted to using the staircase at the end of the hallway outside July and Liberty's room. So Liberty left July sulking in bed, got dressed, and climbed out through the window, down the ladder, across a terrace, down another ladder, and into the kitchen.

There a fire burned in another corner adobe fireplace. Putt sat in a rocker with a cup of coffee. Madeline was standing at an old-fashioned white-enamel gas range. Sure enough, she was flipping pancakes and the sausage was sizzling. But when Liberty looked over at Zanny, she became suspicious.

"What are you stuffing into those blue rags?" she asked.

Zanny was standing at a pine table that held small plates of thinly sliced tomatoes, grated cheese, and some other unidentifiable substances that Liberty feared would be passed off as food.

"They are not blue rags. They are—help me out, Charly and Molly." Zanny looked up at the little twins, who were kneeling on a bench across from her with their elbows on the table.

"Blue tortillas!" Charly and Molly cried out together.

"I've never seen blue tortillas," Liberty said.

"You've never seen white tortillas that didn't come in plastic bags and weren't frozen. These are genuine blue-corn tortillas. They were in our refrigerator, supplied by whoever left the rest of the groceries."

"That would be Marguerite Greyeyes," Putt said. "She is the Ms. Fix-it of the neighborhood, the unofficial mayor, and the owner of the trading post."

"Are we having blue tortillas for breakfast?" Liberty asked, a tone of slight alarm in her voice.

"No, for our picnic," Zanny replied.

"We're going on a picnic?"

"Sure. We've got to reconnoiter the territory, and your dad has work to do, and Aunt Honey's going to run errands with your mom. So I thought you guys would like to go on a picnic."

"And I want to get your mother outfitted," Aunt Honey said.

"Outfitted?" Madeline said. There was a little quaver in her voice as she looked at her twin sister. Putt looked up from his papers at his sister-in-law, blinked, started to say something, and decided not to.

This doesn't sound good, July flashed as he came into the kitchen.

I hope she doesn't decide to bleach her hair like Aunt Honey's, Molly flashed.

It would match those pots. July looked at the burnished copper skillets and pans that hung against the adobe wall.

I think Mom could wear a little more lipstick. I love that orange lipstick Aunt Honey wears, Charly flashed.

I think she's fine just the way she is, Liberty replied.

Yeah, me, too, agreed July.

Madeline was more short than tall, and her untinted hair was cut in a simple style that swung just below her ears.

She sometimes powdered the band of freckles across her nose, but that was the extent of Madeline's makeup. Her twin sister, on the other hand, was tall and had a large mouth, made bigger by bright lipstick. Honey never left the house without makeup—eyelashes thickened with mascara, eyeshadow coordinated to match the colors she was wearing, long polished fingernails that were real and not press-on, spots of rouge on her cheeks, and bleached hair that was stiff with hairspray and sculpted into elaborate shapes. Two bright wings of hair now projected from under her cowboy hat, and a single short braid sprang out from behind. There were never two sisters, let alone twin sisters, as different as Honey and Madeline.

"I just thought I'd take you shopping and get you one of these," Honey said, touching her white cowboy hat, "and a pair of boots, of course."

"Oh . . . er . . . er." Madeline was stammering and shaking her head.

Why doesn't she just come out and say she doesn't want to look like a dork! Liberty fumed.

A pained look crossed Madeline's face, and then she turned and smiled brightly. "You know it looks an awful lot like something out of my next year's recital wear catalog. Wouldn't want to give a sneak preview too far in advance," she said lightly, and laughed.

6.

Coyotes Don't Sleep

THIS IS *a little creepy,* Liberty flashed.

I'll say! July agreed.

Why are those people carrying those signs and looking so angry? Charly wondered.

Yeah, I can read that one. GO HOME STARBUCK, Molly flashed.

Other signs suggested that Putnam Starbuck go fishing, and some showed pictures of the beautiful blue-striped pepper fish. The seven protesters stood on one side of the road that led up to the field office of the Environmental Protection Agency. On the other side, silent but glaring with obvious anger, were at least twenty Pueblo and Navajo people. They, too, carried signs: PEOPLE ARE MORE IMPORTANT THAN FISH and WATER MEANS LIFE.

The children and Zanny had walked to the field office with Putnam because it was next door to the trading post and they needed to get drinks and cookies for their picnic. Now the seven angry white people began to chant, "Hey! Hey! Go away! Save a species; start today!"

"This is awful," Liberty whispered. The little twins huddled close to Zanny. None of the children was used to this—it was terrible and weird. Their father had never been on the unpopular side of an environmental issue.

"Oh dear." Putt sighed and cast a nervous glance at his children.

Suddenly there was a shift in attention and a brief stillness. The Indians drew apart. A large woman stepped forward. She was dressed in a colorful, long, tiered skirt and a velvet blouse, and over the front of the blouse hung heavy silver necklaces. Turquoise-and-silver pendants swung from her ears and a woven scarlet shawl was wrapped around her broad shoulders. She wore her long black hair, streaked with white, in a fat bun.

"*Ya' at' eeh,* Mr. Starbuck." The woman smiled broadly. Relief and pure joy swept over Putt's face.

"Marguerite Greyeyes?"

"Yes, sir." And then she said, as if she were painting with words, "I am Marguerite Greyeyes, born to the Bitter Water Clan and born for the Turning Mountain People." She bent over to look at the children and slapped her bronze cheek. "And these must be your wonderful children. My goodness, am I seeing double?"

"No, we're twins," Charly said softly. She seemed transfixed. Marguerite's shiny silver pendants set with turquoise stones caught the sun, and her dark eyes, neither old nor young, were full of mystery.

She's like a rainbow, Molly flashed.

A living rainbow, July added.

Yes, agreed Liberty.

Sunshine bounced off the silver jewelry and the bright colors of her skirt and blouse until Marguerite Greyeyes seemed wrapped in dazzling light.

"Ah." Her voice was like a gentle, lilting melody. "We like twins here. Twins are special!" She turned to the protesters. "Okay now, you folks!" She waved her hand as if she were shooing away pesky gnats. She walked boldly right up to a young man with a beard. "You go and find something useful to do—really useful." She narrowed her eyes and looked hard at all of them.

"Marguerite," the man with the beard said, "this is useful. You'll see that you just cannot wipe out a species without hurting others."

"We are all linked together," said a woman standing beside him. She wore her long blond hair in braids, like several of the young Indian girls, and had them laced with leather strips that ended in beaded medallions. "We are all part of the sacred web of life."

"Aaaachh!" Marguerite made a sound in the back of her throat. "You know nothing about sacred webs of life. You wrap yourself in Indian blankets when it suits you. For one

hundred years after they put us on this reservation, we didn't even have running water—where were you then? Don't talk to me about sacred webs. You go talk to Spider Woman and learn about the webs of our people. You learn about our gods and their wisdom. Spider Woman, Changing Woman, White Shell Woman, First Woman. You know nothing!" She waved her hand at the protesters once more and they began to move away. She turned to Putt. "Never mind them, Mr. Starbuck. They are like spoiled children. They'll give you no trouble. I know how to handle them."

"So I see," Putt said admiringly.

Marguerite turned to the children. "Come, children. Come, Miss Zanny and Mr. Starbuck. Come into the store."

They followed her through the door into the sun-baked adobe building that housed the Tres Arroyos Trading Post. The walls of the building were almost three feet thick. It was cool inside, and from the immense ceiling beams swung all sorts of goods—clusters of buckets, spools of rope and cable, baskets, bridles, spurs, bright strings of dried red chili peppers and onions. A wall of shelves held Stetson cowboy hats, stacks of flannel shirts, and bolts of the bright velveteen that was used to make the skirts Marguerite and many of the other Navajo women wore. There were canned goods, bread, coffee, tea, and bottles of juice and soda. On the floor were bushel baskets filled with pinto beans and potatoes, and sacks of flour and sugar.

In the center of the room was a large black potbellied

stove. An old man wrapped in a handwoven blanket sat in a rocker by the stove, smoking a pipe. Two snowy white braids dangled from under his black-brimmed, high-crowned hat. A cane hung on the back of the rocker.

Marguerite led the Starbucks to the elderly man, bent over, and spoke Navajo loudly into his ear. She looked at Putnam. "My grandfather, Hosteen Nakai, Mr. Starbuck." The old man looked up but did not see. His nearly color-less, blind eyes seemed to stare out from behind a thick layer of clouds. He reached his hand out and Putt clasped it.

"Sometimes I forget my English." The old man's voice, a leathery whisper, sounded as if it came from far away. "But we are pleased you come to help the Dineh, the People, and the people of the pueblos, too. We are a thirsting people, all of us, the Navajo and Pueblo. You have brought your children?" He lifted his chin higher.

"Yes, yes." Putnam motioned the children to come closer. Marguerite spoke again in Navajo to her grandfather.

"Ah! Ah!" His mouth split into a wide smile. He answered Marguerite in Navajo.

"He wants to meet you and see your faces, if that is okay with you." Marguerite turned toward the children. "He does this by touching your faces with his fingers. He likes twins. Once there were twins in his mother's family, the Mud Clan. He remembers hearing stories of them. This was very long ago because my grandfather is nearly one hundred years old."

"One hundred years old!" None of the four twins had ever met anybody so old. They quickly lined up to have their faces "seen" by the century-old fingers. Hosteen Nakai clenched the pipe in his teeth and with both hands traced the contours of Charly's face. Then he turned to Molly and did the same. As he ran his fingers over their faces, his own face seemed to brighten; it looked as though a light flickered behind the foggy old eyes.

July and Liberty stepped forward. Liberty knew she had never seen such old, wrinkled hands. The veins popped up like cords and the dark skin was mottled with spots. The knuckles, swollen with arthritis, reared up like mountains. The purple veins looked like a network of rivers spreading out toward the wrists, where the skin gathered into deep, wrinkly ridges. These hands seemed as old as the earth and as rugged as the New Mexico landscape. When they touched her face, however, the touch was light and the fingertips smooth.

Liberty saw that the old man's face had suddenly turned serious. The light behind the foggy eyes vanished. He spoke Navajo rapidly in a low whisper. As he shifted his attention to July's face, Liberty watched and tried to fit the shape of his lips to the sound he was making. One thing was clear to Liberty. He either thought that she and July weren't as cute as Charly and Molly, or something was disturbing him about them. What could it be?

The old man grasped their hands, July's left and her

right. Liberty hadn't realized how large Hosteen Nakai's hands were until her and July's hands disappeared within his grip just as if the earth had split open and swallowed up two small creatures. "You be careful," he whispered. "You be very careful." There was no one nearby to overhear. Marguerite was taking Putt and Zanny into the back room to show them her loom, and Molly and Charly had wandered away.

What's he talking about? July flashed.

I don't know, but something about us really upset him.

I didn't think we were that bad-looking!

I don't think it has anything to do with how we look. It's something else, but I don't know what.

Out of the corner of her eye, Liberty caught someone staring at them. Standing in a doorway that led into another room of the trading post was a girl of about nine years old. Hosteen Nakai seemed to sense the little girl, too, for he dropped their hands and called to the child, "Come here, Vera."

This guy's got eyes where we don't see them, Liberty flashed to July.

"Vera, you met these children?" the old man inquired.

"I got their cookies for them for their picnic." She looked shyly at her feet.

"Ah, yes. You scramble up there like Mrs. Spider up her ladder with your young legs. Those cookies are high up. Marguerite keeps them high up so they won't get stolen by coyotes." Vera and the old man laughed. "This is Vera SnowFlower," Hosteen told Liberty and July. "She's learning to be a good potter like her mother and grandmother and great-grandmother and great-great-grandmother. She is from the pueblo of Manteca. Pueblans are good potters. That is their tradition, as weaving is for us, the Navajos."

Vera had the shiniest hair Liberty had ever seen. It was parted in the middle and pulled into two long loose bunches held by beaded medallions with bird figures in the center. Vera's dark eyes were fringed with thick black lashes that reminded Liberty of feathery ferns. The twins invited Vera to join them on their picnic, but she looked at her toes again, shook her head, and murmured that she had to get back to help her mother.

Marguerite, meanwhile, had drawn a rough map for Zanny and the children.

"It's very close to your house on the mesa. You go back there, walk down to the river. You follow it to the bend. You'll see a sign—Cibola Wash. You can cross the river there because it's practically dried up. You go to the other side. You watch out for rattlesnakes." All four twins looked alarmed. "Don't worry. They're getting sleepy this time of year. Just don't reach into any holes or grab for something without looking first. Then you turn north."

"I've got a compass," July said quickly.

"Okay," Marguerite said. "I'll give you a tip, though. In this country, if you ever lose your way and don't have a compass, if you come across a hogan you will know which way is east."

"How?" asked July.

"The door of a hogan always faces east, because that is where the new day begins. Now, after you turn north, you walk for about five minutes, no more, and you'll see Pink Mesa. It won't look pink this time of day—more rusty. That's a great place for a picnic. You'll see this whole land stretch out before you. And who knows what you might find."

"What?" Molly asked.

"Well, you never know, do you?"

The rocking chair creaked, and the leathery voice suddenly spoke.

"But be careful."

"You worry too much, Grandfather. The snakes are sleepy now."

"But the coyotes don't sleep!"

7.

Home Run, the Psychic Hamster

"IT'S NOT pink at all!" Molly said with great emphasis.

"Not right now," Zanny replied. "Remember, she said something about how in the middle of the day it would look red."

"Rusty, not really red," Charly answered. She was holding Home Run in his traveling plastic ball under her arm.

"Girls, I want you to watch Home Run carefully. It won't do if that ball goes rolling down the side of this mesa. It would be one heck of a crash."

"But the ball would protect Home Run so he wouldn't get splattered all over," Molly added, her voice serious as she contemplated Home Run bouncing down the rocky way they had just come up.

They were halfway to the top of the mesa. The distance had been deceiving and the path was steep. At this high altitude, the thin air made Zanny pant; her cheeks were nearly as bright as her copper-colored hair.

Liberty and July had run ahead and were already at the top, with half of the picnic supplies. They had popped open cans of soda and were looking out across the land from the high mesa. In the noon sun the sagebrush and greasewood looked silvery gray, the rocks, deep rugged red. Some were streaked with bands of yellow and gray. A distant mountain climbed into a cloudless blue sky. This was the Land of Plenty of Room. The Land of the Empty. The word *empty* suddenly had a whole new meaning for July and Liberty.

It's as if you could stretch forever here. Liberty's flash was a quiet twinkle through the channels.

He knew exactly what she meant. This was a land so big that only their imaginations could fill it.

Here come the little turkeys, July flashed.

"We heard that, Jelly Bean!" Charly roared. Home Run ran up the inside of the ball she clutched under her arm, froze, and stared at July as Charly marched furiously toward him.

"Yeah, don't call us turkeys, fathead." Molly was right behind Charly.

"I"—there was a pant, a gasp, and a deep groan— "would be happy if someone would call me a turkey." Zanny shifted her backpack as she prepared to climb the last steep incline to the top of the mesa, where all the children were now sitting and looking completely rested.

I feel the Southwest curriculum coming on. It's in the breeze, folks. An educational opportunity, July flashed.

"Yeah, so why is it so great to be a turkey?" Liberty asked, taking out the cookies and starting to unpack the picnic.

"Yeah, why?" asked Molly as she busily opened a tortilla rolled in waxed paper. "I wish this were a Twinkie."

"Turkey was the hero bird in the story your mom read to you. When all those creatures were escaping from the flood to the fifth world, it was Turkey who brought in his wings the most important things of all—the seeds for growing food."

"Ha!" Charly exclaimed.

"Navajo and Pueblo people use his feathers in all their most important ceremonies."

"Yeah, keep calling us turkeys—you . . ." Molly turned to Zanny. "What's the worst thing that you can call someone out here?"

Zanny thought a moment, then took a gulp of soda. "I guess that would be a coyote."

"A coyote?" J. B. asked. He thought of how Hosteen Nakai had warned them about coyotes, but then he remembered that Aunt Honey had worn the little coyote pin with the glittering rhinestone eyes and called the coyote a funny little fellow or something.

"I thought coyotes were supposed to be funny, Zanny," July said.

"No, I don't think they were really funny. Coyote in some stories was just a playful trickster, but he also caused trouble and hardship for people. Coyote could be nasty and mean." The kids were absolutely quiet and still. Even Home Run, whom they had let out to run around on the picnic blanket, stopped, by a bag of chips.

"Coyote, after all, brought death."

"Death!" the children exclaimed.

"Then why was Aunt Honey wearing that pin?" July gasped.

"She probably didn't know."

"Didn't know what?"

"The old story about Coyote." Zanny paused. "Well, there are a few—but it all boils down to one thing: death." She paused again, then spoke quietly. "The fifth world was becoming too crowded. They knew people had to die. It was Coyote who decided it should be forever; it was Coyote who decided where the spirits should go so they could never come back. In some stories it's beneath the waters of a very deep lake; in others, there was to be a grass house. Medicine men would go there and sing to the spirits, calling them back to life. But Coyote caused a whirlwind to come and slam the door forever so that there was no chance of the spirits returning. Coyote made death forever, eternal."

"Forever?" Molly asked.

"You mean ever *and* ever?" Charly said.

It was hard for the little twins to understand that death was forever. It was a big idea even for Liberty and July.

"Yes," Zanny said. "And now, according to the old stories, some people believe that whenever anyone meets a whirlwind or hears the wind's whistle, it is really the soul of a dead person caught somewhere between the spirit land and the land of the living, wandering the earth, trying to find a place to go."

A shiver ran through Liberty like the memory of a distant wind. For the first time in several days, she thought of the rustle of dry leaves at her window back in Washington. And hadn't there been another sound—a whisper—embedded within the scraping?

"Where's Home Run?" Charly's shriek split Liberty's thoughts.

"Oh no!" Molly wailed. "Coyotes got him!" Within two seconds there was a full-scale alert, with both little twins howling.

"Is he in the chips?" Zanny asked, grabbing the bag and shaking out its contents.

They quickly searched the picnic remnants. Liberty unrolled the two remaining tortillas—Home Run loved tomatoes, especially when they were sliced thin the way Zanny had cut them. They tore open the chocolate-chip-cookie bag to see if the hamster had gone in for the last crumbs.

The big thermos of water was propped against Zanny's backpack. Could he have crawled in it and . . .

Drowned! The word exploded in the telepathic channels. Molly grabbed the thermos and poured out the water.

"What are you doing!" Zanny cried. "You do *not* pour out water in the desert—survival rule number one. Are you guys crazy?"

But there was still no Home Run and now no water. Zanny searched through her backpack. No Home Run.

"Okay," Zanny said seriously. "I want us to use the buddy system and all stay within sight and sound of each other."

This precaution seemed slightly ridiculous to Liberty. How far could a little hamster go? And even if he had gone far, how could they ever find such a little creature in all this vastness? This was, after all, the Land of the Empty, and at the moment, it seemed empty of Home Run. In mute testimony to this fact, the hamster's clear plastic ball stood glaringly empty in the bright New Mexico sunshine. Home Run could have crawled into any one of the million little crevices and holes. Rattlesnakes would delight in the rare, exquisite taste of a pet-store hamster.

Ten minutes later, July cried out jubilantly, "Holy moley! I got him!" July had gone more than halfway down the mesa and found the hamster under a small ledge. "And look what Home Run's got!" The others came racing down to where July was crouched.

"Don't reach for anything you can't see, J. B. Remember what Marguerite said," Zanny warned.

But it was no rattlesnake that Home Run had found, nor was it a coyote. July held up something flat. It was shaped like a jagged butterfly, but the design on its wings was a bold geometric pattern unlike that of any butterfly.

"It's a pottery shard!" Zanny's voice swelled with excitement. "July, this is terrific. An artifact! You found a genuine artifact!"

"I didn't find it. Home Run did!" July hoisted the hamster up in the air.

"Hooray for Home Run! Hooray!" Charly and Molly cried.

"I wonder what it's from," July said. They all gathered around him and examined the fragment.

"It's more curved—concave—than I thought when you first held it up," Zanny observed. "Maybe it was part of a bowl, or a pitcher.

"It's still so bright. Are you sure it's old?"

"Well, I'm not sure. We'll have to find out."

"Can we keep it?" Charly asked.

"No, no. It's not ours to keep."

"But finders keepers, losers weepers," July said.

"Not in this case," Zanny said firmly. "It's a big problem out here."

"What's a big problem?" Liberty asked.

"Pothunters. These things belong to the Indians who

live here. They do not belong to white people or anybody who comes in to take them and sell them. And a lot of people have been doing that. It's illegal, but they still do it. It would be just like someone going into your house in Washington and taking something old. Maybe it's even broken, but it still has meaning for you—maybe it belonged to your grandma out in Kansas and she gave it to your mom. Nobody has the right to come in and take it. That's stealing. We'll take it into the trading post and Marguerite Greyeyes will know what to do with it."

"I wonder if there are any more pieces," July said.

Everyone dropped to their hands and knees and began crawling around to look for more. Just as Liberty was saying, "Nope. I think that was the last piece!" July shouted. "I don't believe it!"

"Did you find something?"

"I didn't, but look who did!"

Home Run was emerging from under a flat rock, nosing in front of him another fragment of pottery.

"Our little Home Run!" cooed Charly.

"He's a genius!" squealed Molly.

"An archaeologist!" exclaimed Zanny.

"He's psychic," July said, holding Home Run close to his face and peering into the rodent's squinty little eyes. "We've got a psychic hamster here, no doubt about it."

8.

The Mystery of the Left-Handed Potter

THE TWINS were brimming with excitement and talking loudly as they walked up the path to the trading post. They hardly noticed the two protesters who were still hanging around under the shade of a cottonwood tree.

"I don't see why Liberty gets to carry the pot pieces," Molly whined.

"The older twins always get to do everything," Charly grumped.

"Quit arguing," Zanny scolded. "You should be thrilled that we have discovered these ancient pottery fragments. "Now we're going to go into the Post and Marguerite might be able to tell us all about them. So just be quiet and listen."

Five minutes later they were listening quietly as Marguerite Greyeyes turned one of the fragments over in her hand. "So, you see. You can tell that this painting was done by a brush made from a yucca plant. The bristles are very long and straight—good for this kind of work." She was a person to whom all artifacts were brought and reported; she would contact the proper authorities for the region.

Hosteen Nakai was still in his rocker by the potbellied stove. They had all thought he was snoozing until his leathery voice spoke in Navajo.

"Ah, yes!" Marguerite replied. "My grandfather says I should take out the magnifying glass and show you that you can see how the bristles all lie flat against the surface when the potter paints the lines of this pot. My grandfather, before his eyes failed him, was an expert in reading the signs of these pots—the designs, the kind of paint used, even the way potters had held the pots while they worked on them. He could tell the history of a pot from the smallest shards, much smaller than these."

Marguerite held the fragments for them as each Starbuck child looked through the magnifying glass that she had brought out from behind the counter. "You can even tell that this potter painted with the left hand and not the right. See how the lines end—that one in particular. It's a little broader at the finish of the stroke."

Vera SnowFlower came through the doorway. "Ah, Vera, come here," Marguerite said. "See these nice pottery fragments the children found. Old Anasazi pieces and a left-handed potter like you."

Vera came over to the counter and looked at the pieces. "Ahh," she said in quiet admiration.

"Yeah, nice work," Marguerite agreed. "Someday you'll be this good, Vera."

"It's mineral paint," Vera said, touching a fragment lightly.

"Yes," said Marguerite. "Still so nice and shiny. And you know what I must do now, children?"

"What?" Charly and Molly said in unison.

"Call Dr. Ridley at the university. He is interested in all pottery pieces from the Anasazi times that might have been done by a left-handed potter, especially one who used mineral paints. Nowadays we know which potter from which pueblo does which piece. We know that Vera's mother makes her own designs in a particular way, and we know that Vera herself makes the rabbits on her pots a special way. But although there are many styles of ancient pottery, it has never been possible to tell which person did a piece or started a new style. Always it has been as if the old Anasazi potters were without faces, without names." Marguerite paused. "But it was my grandfather who began to understand, just about the time the blindness came, that there might be one potter, one individual potter who was very much better than all the rest, whose style was recognizable. This individual was left-handed and often used mineral paints. This person was a master!" Marguerite's eyes had a faraway look, as if she were trying to peer through the mists of centuries into the past. "Archaeologists," she continued, "are very interested in this idea. If they could discover who this person was, one of the Ancient Ones would be known. One of those lost might be found."

"Would it solve the mystery of what happened to the Anasazi?" July asked. He looked toward Hosteen Nakai, but the old man seemed to be asleep. The low angle of the setting sun spilled a path of light directly through the doorway onto the rocker.

"Perhaps it would not solve the mystery, but it would at least make the Ancient Ones seem just a little bit closer . . . which would not be bad." Marguerite smiled.

Closer . . . Liberty imagined walking in giant steps across the emptiness of the land, trying to get closer.

Closer to what? July teleflashed.

I don't know . . . The mystery potter . . . What do you think—was it a girl or a boy?

Or a man or a woman?

I don't know.

"Some people," Marguerite said, "believe that there is a spirit in the clay, even in the broken pieces." She held up the two fragments. A shadow passed across the doorway, slicing through the path of sunlight. Hosteen Nakai stirred in his rocker as the sweep of shade crossed his face. "Pieces like these can still have the spirit in them, and some believe that if you listen carefully enough you can hear, like a faint voice, the spirit songs of the wind moving through the ancient vessels and their broken pieces."

That night, before bed, Liberty and July once again crawled up the ladder onto the roof. They wore their winter parkas over their pajamas, for even though it was just the first week in October, the night was cold. The wintery pinch in the air snapped their cheeks pink. Chilly gusts blew through their hair and the sky was bright with stars.

Madeline poked her head through the skylight. "My last night—want another story?" She would be leaving early the next day for Washington, D.C.

"Sure," the twins answered.

"You know," Madeline said as they came down the ladder, "it can snow early out here. They say that you can wake up one morning and everything is white. It could happen before the first of November." The children took off their coats and crawled under their blankets. "Okay, we left off when the first people had just scratched their way through the hole in the dome of the sky to the next world, trying to outrun the flood that Water Monster had sent out to get them. 'Little did they know . . . ,'" Madeline read, "'that the reason for Water Monster's anger was Coyote . . .'"

Coyote again, July teleflashed.

"'Coyote had stolen Water Monster's twin babies,'" Madeline continued.

Twins nonetheless, Liberty flashed in reply.

Kidnapped twins!

Madeline read on. "'When First Man and First Woman discovered this, they made Coyote hand over the babies, then sent them back to Water Monster. Peace was temporarily restored. First Woman decided it was time to put the stars in the sky. She laid out chips of sparkling quartz on a blanket and made a plan for the design of the constellations and the movement of the stars. The designs of her beautiful jewelry were to be the laws of the Navajo world— telling people when to hunt, when to plant, when to come together to celebrate. Then Coyote came to help her hang the star jewels in the sky, but he became impatient and swept up the star blanket and shook it fiercely, scattering the bits of stars and stardust all over the blackness of the night sky.'"

That doesn't seem so bad. Liberty yawned and flashed sleepily to July. *It would be kind of pretty seeing the star blanket swirl up into the air flinging out all the stars.*

But July had gone to sleep. By the time Madeline finished the story of Coyote and the stars, Liberty was asleep as well. Madeline kissed them each once and crept out of the bedroom.

A crescent moon swung high into the sky and hung overhead, framed by Liberty and July's skylight. A shaft of silvery light spilled across the tile floor. Liberty was having a confusing dream. Back at Starbuck Recital Wear, her mother was in a marketing meeting with her design team, but instead of dance tutus they were designing a star blanket. Liberty herself was sewing on the sequins.

"No, put it there," one person was saying.

"No, over there—you have too many on that side."

Then Aunt Honey stamped her foot. "Nobody is listening to me. You're doing it all wrong."

"But Aunt Honey, that is where the North Star goes. There always has to be a North Star."

"Oh, nonsense." And she plucked up the North Star from where Liberty had placed it.

Then Liberty got so mad that she snatched up the blanket and hurled it across the meeting room and everybody screamed, "Bad girl! Bad girl!" Even the little coyote pin on Aunt Honey's vest shrieked at her, laughing and screaming, "Bad girl!" Then a long, loping shadow stretched across her dream, and suddenly there was a howl that split the night.

Liberty sat bolt upright in bed. "What are you doing up?" She looked across the room in amazement at her brother.

"Your dreams." July paused. "But then I heard something."

"Like a howl?"

"Yes."

"You mean I didn't dream that animal sound?"

"I don't think so . . ." July scratched his head. "No, no, I'm sure I really heard it out loud."

Liberty switched abruptly to the telepathic channels. *Let's go up the ladder and see if we can see anything out there— a coyote, maybe. Or do you think it could have been a wolf?*

I don't know, but let's go up.

They pulled on thick socks and their winter parkas, turned up their collars, and scrambled up the ladder.

They stood on the very edge of the roof and looked out into the night. The ridgeline of the jagged mountains stood out blacker than the black of the night.

Well, do you see any animals out here? Liberty asked. July squinted hard. It was just too dark, too long before the dawn, and the moon with its halo of ice crystals seemed veiled and dim.

Naw. Let's go to bed. It's too cold out here.

The twins descended the ladder once more. The fire had nearly gone out, so July added a log. This time they both fell fast asleep.

Across Pinto Wash and down the road near the trading post, another long, loping shadow stretched across an adobe wall. Inside, Hosteen Nakai turned over in his sleep and moaned slightly.

9.

Saddle Up!

JULY HEARD it first. A soft sound filtered through his dreams like a cheerful beckoning call. He opened his eyes and heard it again. In two seconds he was out of bed, across the room, and leaning out the window.

"Oh, wow!" Five pinto ponies stood just outside the gate of the walled courtyard.

"Oh, wow! I'll say." Putt looked up. "I thought you guys would never get up."

"Are they for us, Dad . . . to keep?"

"To keep while we're out here," Putt said. "We're renting them from a cousin of Marguerite Greyeyes. Marguerite thought you kids and Zanny needed a way to get around—you know, to some of the roadless places."

"The roadless places"—July liked the sound of that.

"Is your sister up yet?"

July turned around. Liberty was still sleeping soundly, her mouth hanging open, as though she were recovering from a night of harrowing dreams.

"No," July called down to his father. "But this is worth waking her up for."

All four twins had ridden at their grandmother's farm in Heart's Full, Kansas, so it didn't take them long to get accustomed to riding the ponies. Liberty's and July's ponies were black-and-white. July's had a lightning-bolt–shaped line on its forehead, and Liberty's had an almost totally black face except for an irregularly shaped white star around its left eye. These two ponies became Lightning and Star Eye. Charly's and Molly's had dark red-brown patches that almost matched their own hair. The younger twins had a more difficult time settling on their ponies' names. Between breakfast and lunch, when they had all taken a ride toward Pink Mesa, the little twins had changed their minds at least four times. They had started with Patches and Rags and then gone on to Chip and Chop, which led to Nacho and Dorito. Dorito made them think of their grandma, whose name was Doris, and when they thought of Doris, they of course thought of their own mother, who had left hours before to be driven to the airport by Aunt Honey. So by lunchtime the little twins were settled on Doris and Madeline, trotting behind Lightning and Star Eye.

Why do they always do this? Madeline was the name of their goldfish in London, and their chameleon in Pelican Key. Now they've got Grandma in there, too! I mean who ever heard of naming horses after your mom and grandmother? Liberty flashed.

It could have been worse. Remember their Ken and Barbie days? July flashed back. Luckily the little twins seemed so absorbed in riding that they did not pick up on the telepathic transmissions of their older brother and sister. There had been a time when Charly and Molly had named all their pets after their Ken and Barbie dolls. Home Run himself had spent a humiliating and terrifying first day in the Starbuck household as Ken. Charly and Molly decided to give the hamster a ride in the pink plastic Cadillac that Ken and Barbie went on dates in. Poor old Home Run had taken off down the driveway and nearly met his end as Mrs. Braverman drove down the street. They quickly changed his name, and Putnam had bought the plastic ball as a safer method of transport.

Zanny, who was in the lead on her pony, Jack, turned around. "What do you guys say we try a new place today for our picnic, since we were at Pink Mesa yesterday?"

"Where?" July asked.

"Well, if we stay on this side of the river, there is supposed to be a trail that leads up that rimrock on the edge of the other mesa." She pointed toward a long mesa with a saddleback swoop in the middle. The high-noon sun had leached the color from the rock, which appeared chalky now against the deep blue sky. At the base of the mesa was a band of thick timber.

They ate lunch in the shadow of the rimrock and then went wading in the seep, which was about one inch deep. Charly and Molly smeared their faces with the red mud and played beauty spa; Aunt Honey had told them that mud facials and mud baths were the rage at Rancho Eleganza.

July and Liberty borrowed Home Run to try out his abilities in finding pottery shards and other artifacts, but they had no luck. Either Home Run was not a psychic hamster or there was nothing to discover in this spot. July scooped up Home Run and put him back in the plastic ball. He held the ball up and looked deeply into it the way a fortune-teller might look into a crystal ball. "I believe in you, Home Run! There's just nothing here. That's why you couldn't find it, but I do believe that you are the Psychic Hamster Extraordinaire!"

"Oh, Jelly Bean!" Liberty laughed. "You're getting worse than Dad about Home Run."

After dropping off Home Run and the picnic supplies at home, the children rode over to the trading post to buy some jawbreakers. As soon as they walked in and saw Marguerite's troubled face, they knew something had happened. She told them the disturbing news of the previous night's break-in.

"What?" July said, stunned. He slipped the immense

fiery red jawbreaker to one side of his mouth until his cheek pouched like a chipmunk's.

"Stolen," Liberty said, echoing her brother's disbelief. "The pottery fragments are really gone?"

Marguerite solemnly pulled open the drawer under the cash register where she had kept them. The twins leaned over the counter. The drawer was empty. The shards were gone.

"So where is Home Run when we need him?" Liberty said mournfully.

10.

Blue Doors, Bone Beads, and Witches

SOMEONE HAD slipped into the trading post the previous night and taken the shards. Marguerite had never thought to lock them up. It wasn't that people didn't steal things from the store, but if they did, it was usually money or goods. And if the thieves were pothunters, they usually went out and dug the stuff up themselves—whole pots. Two very small pieces of broken pottery had little value on the black market of Indian artifacts. They would have informational, not monetary, value for a scholar like Dr. Ridley, who would have seen how they fitted together with other pieces that had been brought to him. It was very mysterious. And it was not good.

Marguerite shook her head. "My grandfather would say that the spirits of the pottery have been offended and that trouble will come. I just don't understand it. For a person to steal these—it's just stupid. They could not have known where they came from, where you kids found them—unless . . ." A shadow swept across her eyes.

"Unless what?" Liberty and July asked at once.

"Nothing," Marguerite said quickly.

She doesn't think we stole them, does she? July flashed.

No, of course not, silly. It's obvious what she thinks.

What—what's so obvious? I'm not getting it.

She thinks someone saw where we found them, followed us there.

To Pink Mesa when we had our picnic?

Yes.

I don't think so. I really think that's a long shot, Liberty. Even if they had followed us, how would they know that we had found these fragments? It wasn't like we were screaming at the top of our lungs about it. And there's no place to hide up there on that mesa. We would have seen anyone a mile away.

Yeah, I guess you're right. And it was really Home Run who found the pieces.

The entire telepathic transmission took place within two blinks of an eye. And although the twins were sure that Marguerite did not suspect them, and they could not imagine anyone actually following them to Pink Mesa, a strange disquiet began to seep around the edges of their brains and trickle down their backbones. The feeling was profoundly disturbing and they knew it would grow, that it would niggle at them constantly and never give them a moment's peace.

For the umpteenth time that day, Marguerite searched the drawer where she had put the pottery fragments. Then she gasped and stared into the palm of her hand. There between the two long creases, the ones fortune-tellers call the heart line and the life line, was a small white bead.

"A bead," July said.

"A bone bead," Marguerite said in a barely audible whisper. Then, quickly, "Don't say anything to Hosteen Nakai."

"What is it?" pressed Liberty.

"Oh . . . oh, it's nothing."

"Why mustn't he know?"

"Oh, you know." Marguerite laughed slightly, but the laughter in the back of her throat sounded more like rocks cracking than a jolly sound. "You know these old Navajo; they're very superstitious."

"About what?"

"I have heard," Zanny said carefully, "that older Navajo people sometimes believe in those old witchcraft stories . . . What do they call them?" Zanny made the subject sound more like part of the Southwest curriculum than an actual danger. Marguerite seemed to pick up on her tone and relaxed.

"Yes, you are referring to the 'skinwalkers.' That's what they called the witches. The bead was kind of like a bad spell the witches cast. I think somebody's trying to pull our leg here by taking the pottery shards and leaving this." She peered down at the bead again. Although her tone of voice was even, her eyes looked nervous.

"Why'd they call them skinwalkers?" Liberty asked.

"They were thought to be a special kind of witch. They could fly through the air, run as fast as the wind, change into animals—dogs, wolves, coyotes."

"Coyotes," Liberty and July said together.

"Most often they would say that skinwalkers changed into wolves, and that probably came from the old Navajo shepherds' custom of taking the skin of a wolf and disguising themselves in order to surprise herds of sheep or cattle. These old beliefs die hard." Marguerite sighed and then smiled slightly. "You children know why the doors and window frames of your house on the mesa are painted blue?"

"No, why?" Molly piped up. She and Charly had passed up the jawbreakers and had been occupied selecting their ten cents' worth of penny candy.

"Because the old belief is that blue keeps the witches away. Funny, isn't it? But a pretty color."

Not to mention that the door to the trading post and all of its window frames are painted blue, too! Liberty flashed.

Yeah, I think she's trying to change the subject. She still seems pretty nervous about this bead thing, July replied.

And if it was true that the person who had taken the pottery had left the bead, then perhaps that person wanted more than just broken pottery.

11.

The Way of
the Flute Player

"PLEASE, ZANNY, can't we just go out to Pink Mesa? It's a quick ride on the ponies," Liberty pleaded. Since the theft of the pottery shards, the twins were almost desperate to get to Pink Mesa. Perhaps there were more shards, more fragments. And if there were, maybe it would help lead to the identity of the left-handed potter.

"Yeah," said July. "If it took us half an hour to walk—"

"More like forty-five minutes," Zanny said.

"Well, even if it took us fifty minutes to walk, it would take half that time to ride. Come on, Zanny."

"You heard what Hosteen Nakai said. This is big country, harsh country."

"Zanny, it's broad daylight. It's hours before sunset. You can see Pink Mesa from our house."

"You can see the San Francisco Peaks from our house, too, which are hundreds of miles away."

"Therefore, you can see us from here," reasoned Liberty.

The older twins were experts at wearing down adults through an imaginative mixture of fractured logic and persistence. When they pulled out their double-whammy arsenal of persuasive techniques, Liberty and July were an unbeatable combination. And it was double-barreled and double-powered when the little twins got in on the act—then it was truly double trouble squared. Zanny knew it was best to quit now before Charly and Molly joined in. So she capitulated. But she did insist that Liberty and July wear the cowboy hats their father had bought them for sun protection. July was about to protest when Liberty flashed, *The hats are great. I'll tuck in Home Run. He'll have a nice view from the brim, and we need him.*

So ten minutes later Zanny was watching Liberty and July recede into the distance as their ponies followed the river. They were two thin figures erect in their saddles. Against the bright blue sky the figures became sticks on pinto smudges, and as the sticks whittled down to slivers, the smudges became two dark dots. Soon there were only two specks in the distance. Oh dear, Zanny thought, have I made a mistake in letting them go? The specks vanished as the river took a deep turn and pitched down a steep grade.

It's the flute player, Kokopelli! The announcement shimmered through the telepathic channels. With her index finger, Liberty traced the outline of the humpbacked figure, carved in the rock face centuries before. On his stick legs, with his stick arms holding the flute, the figure bent over and played his mute stone melody. The round head at the end of his stick neck curved toward the ground.

The children had gone a little past Pink Mesa because they had spotted some petroglyphs on the rocks beyond. The figure that Liberty now traced had been at the base of a hogback ridge that rose from the flat scrubby ground a few hundred feet away from the mesa.

Liberty, flashed July, *you won't believe this!*

What? Liberty looked to where July was pointing. *Oh my gosh!*

It was another flute player, pointing his flute straight ahead.

It must be a sign, Liberty reasoned.

Of course, flashed July.

They had a strangely familiar feeling. They had felt this sensation before—first in London, in the house in the mews where they had perceived the glimmerings of the ghost Shadrach Holmes, the long-forgotten twin brother of Sherlock Holmes. They'd felt it again in the Florida Keys, when the dolphins had called to them with the strange clicks that penetrated the telepathic channels. Were they being called again?

"Let's just go up and look at it. This path goes right up there," Liberty said aloud.

So they climbed back on their ponies and began to follow the hogback trail up to the second flute player. A wind curled out from behind a boulder, scraping across the flute player's back. Liberty suddenly recalled the sound of dry leaves rustling against the screen of her bedroom window back in Washington.

The way grew steeper, but the path was clear as they followed the stone pictures up the hogback ridge. The hogback's profile against the sky was more like a stegosaurus than a pig. On its crest, eroded rocks jabbed at the sky like spikes, and the rocks were heavily incised with the ancient markings of the vanished people. Beneath the path, wind and water had worn away the land so that the flanks of the hogback slid steeply to the flat country below. Scatterings of tiny flowers—of yellow snakeweed blossoms and the pink quiver of a late-growing evening primrose—clung to the thin crumbly soil with threadlike roots. Liberty watched the blossoms tremble in the breeze as they rode by. She had never thought of flowers as being courageous before, but to grow here, she thought, one had to be. The flowers gave her heart as she and her brother followed the signs of the flute players that now seemed to dance to silent music across every rock.

The hogback dipped down on the other side and trailed into a boulder-strewn wash where a river had once flowed. July thought they had lost the flute player in the wash, but on the far side, he spotted another. Soon they were winding up another mesa—and this one appeared almost blood-red in the setting sun.

The small canyon at the base of this mesa was where the children had first noticed the rocks with the odd, gaping holes—some large enough to stand up straight in, others just big enough to sit in if you curled up tight. *They look like they've been blown out,* Liberty flashed.

They probably were. I bet these were volcanic rocks. Bubbling gases and lava could have popped these holes, July replied.

To Liberty, the holes looked like mouths, ready to sing, talk, or tell a tale—like the mouths on the storyteller figures that Marguerite Greyeyes sold at the trading post. The storyteller figures came from the Cochiti Pueblo tradition. Dozens of small children gathered around a seated man or woman, whose mouth was open as he or she sang or told a tale. Liberty had an odd feeling that these dark, gaping holes had stories to tell.

As they rode past the last big rock before the summit of the mesa, there was yet another figure of the flute player. This time Kokopelli was in a new position. He lay on his back, as if at rest, with his flute pointed toward the sky. July and Liberty urged Lightning and Star Eye to the summit of the long, broad mesa, and the ponies broke into a trot.

"Hold up a second," Liberty said. While July had been calculating distance, Liberty had been surveying the lay of the land. Beneath the hissing of the yellow senna and the quivering of the needlegrass, a curious geometry emerged from the earth. Liberty stopped Star Eye and looked down and around, following an imaginary perimeter of which she was the center. It was not her imagination. The land lifted here. They were on top of a hump, and the strange thing about this hump was that it was perfectly . . .

And I mean perfectly, she flashed, *round!*

Liberty's right, July thought. Leave it to Liberty to see the overall shape of things. July was better with the bits and pieces, but Liberty could always detect the pattern.

Liberty reached up and slipped Home Run out of her hat and into her shirt pocket, then dismounted Star Eye and began to walk around the circle. It was about fifty feet across. She gently tamped the earth with her boot. Home Run seemed agitated. His sharp little toenails dug through her pocket as he climbed out onto her shoulder.

July. His name seemed to glow like an ember in the channels. This was serious. *July,* Liberty flashed again. *I have an announcement to make. We are standing on top of a kiva, no doubt a very ancient kiva.* As if to confirm this archaeological discovery, Home Run ran down Liberty's leg and onto the ground. There was a gritty, skittering sound near her feet, and Home Run slid out of sight where a small pocket of earth had given way.

"He's gone!" July cried.

"Buried alive!" screamed Liberty. She rushed forward.

"Get back! Get back! This whole thing could go!" July shouted. "We've got to get out of this circle!"

Liberty realized immediately that July was right. There could be an avalanche of dirt that would swallow them all up—July, Liberty, Lightning, and Star Eye. They rushed the ponies outside the circle. Looking back, they could see only a small dimple in the circle at the spot where Home Run had been swallowed by the kiva.

"Now what do we do?" Liberty moaned.

"Poor Home Run." July sighed. "You know Charly and Molly are just going to kill us if we come home without him."

"We've got to figure out a way to get to him. We've just got to." Liberty bit her lip as she thought. She had looked at a book on kivas at their house. She tried to remember what these special rooms were like. She had recalled their shape—round.

Think about the inside of it, Liberty, July flashed.

Well, they're round.

But how do you get in them—without killing yourself, that is?

Yes, that could be a problem. Liberty was trying very hard to remember the layout of the kivas, where the people had gathered for religious ceremonies. How did they get inside? Why, she realized, just the way Home Run had— through the roof hole, with a ladder. But that could be very dangerous here. The entire roof might cave in and they would be buried alive.

Don't even think of it, Liberty. It's insane. No hamster is worth it. Not even a psychic one. It's really dangerous. There must be another way into this kiva. Think, Liberty. Was a roof hole the only way to get in?

No, no. I think I read somewhere that they could be entered through small tunnels in the kiva walls . . . but . . . She paused and looked around. It was hard to imagine where walls or tunnels might be. *We'd better start looking for an alternative way.*

She climbed back on Star Eye and began guiding him slowly toward the edge of the mesa where she could look down the rock face to its base. But there was nothing that suggested a tunnel or entrance, just land sloping away, gently spotted with puffy juniper shrubs and a band of ponderosa pines below that. Across a dry riverbed was another band of lighter green where the cottonwoods grew. The light was changing, and Liberty knew they would have to head home very soon or Zanny would never let them out again. A trap-door spider emerged from under the ground. *So you're down there, too!* Liberty thought as she watched the spider climb out from under the trapdoor it had constructed of little clods of dirt and pebbles. It was definitely time to get home if these spiders were coming out for their twilight hunt. Soon the bats would be swooping through the sky just before the moon rose.

We've got to go now, July, or we're in big trouble. Don't worry, we'll think of something.

As they rode off Liberty turned to look over her shoulder. The mesa looked like a drop of blood against the darkening desert sky.

12.

Dinner Disaster

LIBERTY AND JULY made it back to the house minutes before Zanny and the little twins did. There had been just enough time to scrape the sweat off their ponies, rub them down, and give them buckets of water before Charly and Molly had come roaring in on Doris and Madeline, talking a mile a minute. They had been to Vera SnowFlower's pueblo. They had seen her and her mother make pottery, beautiful pottery. Vera was teaching them how to do it. They had each made a little pinch pot that would be fired.

"And do you know how they build the fire?" Molly asked.

"Outdoors with poop!" Charly said, her eyes wide.

"Poop?" said July. "What kind of poop?"

"Cow poop and sheep poop. And do you know what happens if the poop gets right on the pottery?"

"No, what happens?"

Nothing like a little bathroom talk to keep these twerps pleasantly distracted, Liberty thought. She was careful not to let the idea of Home Run roll into the telepathic channels.

"Well," Molly was saying, swelling with self-importance over her newfound knowledge, "if a cow pie or something gets on the pot or bowl or whatever is being cooked up in the fire, it makes a big, dark smudge. They call it a fire cloud. Vera sometimes makes it part of the design."

"It depends on the pot," Charly said.

"Oh, that's very interesting," July said in a slow, warm voice, making it sound as though this were the most interesting thing he had ever heard.

But how could they think about fire clouds when poor Home Run was trapped in a kiva? Liberty thought. She hoped he was just trapped and not already dead!

July flopped down on his bed. "All I ever wanted or needed to know about pottery."

"I know," Liberty said. "But you did an excellent job of distracting the twins."

"It bought us a little time, Liberty, but not much. What are we going to do?"

Liberty switched to the telepathic channels. July felt what was coming.

There's only one thing to do!

I was afraid you were going to say that.

I haven't said it yet, Jelly Bean.

One doesn't need a crystal ball to figure it out.

Well, just be happy that Mom's in Washington and that Dad and Zanny are heavy sleepers.

So when do we saddle up?

Just as soon as they all conk out. In the meantime, we've got to read all we can about kivas and figure out how to get into this one.

July looked out the window. A pale disk was just rising over the blue mountains. *It's going to be a full moon tonight. That will help.*

"Dinner!" Zanny called.

Now, if we can only get through dinner without Charly and Molly asking about Home Run, July flashed.

The entire family was so ravenous, they barely opened their mouths for anything except shoveling in the tortillas stacked with beans, lettuce, and tomatoes. The little twins slurped down hot corn soup and asked for seconds.

"Doing pottery makes you hungry," Charly said.

"And tired." Molly yawned.

July looked hopefully at Liberty.

"We'll clear; you just stay there," Liberty said.

"You want some dessert, kids?" Putnam said. "I brought home some chocolate ice cream and syrup and some whipped cream in a squirt can."

"Oooh."

"Yum."

But by the time Liberty and July returned with the ice cream, Charly and Molly had fallen fast asleep. Their little red heads rested on their place mats, and their hands, adorned with acid-green press-on nails, rested lightly on the tabletop.

Zanny and Putnam each picked up a twin and headed upstairs to tuck them in. Just as Zanny was rounding the corner with Molly, she turned to Liberty and July. "By the way," she whispered, "where's Home Run?"

Lie!

The word flashed a putrid shade of yellow in the channels.

"Oh, upstairs," Liberty said casually.

"Yeah, we thought we'd take him up some of these left-over tortillas. He really loves all this Mexican food."

"He's a dear," Zanny said. "I never thought I could really care for a rodent, but you know I really love Home Run. He's got such wonderful—it sounds silly, but really a wonderful personality. Imagine loving tortillas after that pet-store hamster food all these months. A marvelous adjustment."

Oh, good grief! Liberty wailed in the channels. *I hope he's adjusting to life in the kiva!*

You know, I think this is the first time we've ever lied out-right to Zanny. July flashed.

Not really, Liberty replied. *We've certainly stretched things before. We've kind of bent the facts a little bit and sneaked around.*

Whatever! It feels rotten. July telesighed.

They sat at the table and twiddled their spoons in the puddles of chocolate.

I'm not really hungry anymore, Liberty flashed.

Me, neither.

13.

A Flute Call in the Night

"'THE LARGE ceremonial rooms known as kivas, where special ceremonies and rituals were held, varied from pueblo to pueblo. Usually round and often underground, these chambers were the center of spiritual life in the community. The kivas were most often entered by ladders or stairs leading through a roof entrance. A kiva at a cliff dwelling might be entered through an opening in the wall.'" Liberty looked up from the book she was reading aloud. "So you see, J.B., there is at least a chance for another way into that place."

July was Googling kivas on his laptop. The twins had told Zanny that they were very interested in the ancient architecture of the cliff pueblos, and particularly in kiva construction. Zanny had been so pleased with their enthusiasm for the Southwest curriculum that she had pointed out several websites on these subjects.

July read, "'Within the kivas the most sacred objects were placed. In the floor of the kiva there was always a small hole called a sipapu. It was believed that the sipapu was the place through which the spirits passed to enter the kiva . . .' Just like the Air Spirit People who crawled out of the Dark World into the Blue and then the Yellow World."

Zanny poked her head into the bedroom. "It's getting late, kids, and you've had a big day."

"Oh, Zanny," Liberty exclaimed. "We're learning so much. Do you know about the sipapus?"

"The whats?" Zanny's blue eyes grew brighter. What a joy it was to have such smart, enthusiastic learners as these Starbuck kids.

Liberty reported their findings.

"Brilliant! Brilliant! You children are wonders." Zanny beamed.

"Listen to this," July said suddenly. "'In many kivas, especially those made in rock and lacking a roof entrance, a small smoke hole was drilled.'" July looked straight at Liberty. His gray eyes turned cool and penetrating.

Smoke hole! Get it, Liberty?

Got it! Perfect hamster-sized hole for guess who to fall through!

Brilliant deduction, Watson.

Oh, no, Holmes—it was you!

Zanny sensed that the children had switched to the telepathic channels.

"Well, kids, don't stay up too late."

Ha!

Well, July, let's just think of it as not staying up late but getting up early.

"Night, Zanny."

"Night, Zanny."

"Night, Liberty. Night, J.B."

As Zanny closed the door, July reached for his Sherlock Holmes deerstalker hat, a hat as precious to him as the coonskin caps were to the little twins. Liberty got up and went for the meerschaum pipe. It helped her think just to suck on it.

So with the props of detection at hand, the Starbuck twins began to think, to deduce another entrance into the kiva.

The game is afoot, Liberty flashed.

The game is a hamster!

But the day had been long and the meal filling, even without the ice-cream sundaes. There had been riding across the desert and lying through their teeth. There had been hamsters swallowed by the earth and humpbacked flute players with melodies trapped in stone.

Liberty and July Starbuck fell sound asleep. They had closed the skylight against the chill, and the blossoms that had cascaded through the opening on previous nights now scratched on the glass. The moon rose huge and silver in the sky. The northwest wind blew sharper, stinging with sand. Wrapped within the stinging wind was a lonely, hollow sound. It was a strange, unearthly music, aching in its desolation and eerie in its beauty. And like the Air Spirit People on their way from that first dark place to the earth's surface, the notes climbed through a tunnel in the wind and floated into the children's bedroom in the house high on the mesa.

Liberty dreamed of Spider Woman flying on Dragonfly through the crack in the thin dome of the sky. The insect's wings suddenly gathered together as Dragonfly's body arched and humped up. From his face a flute grew. The strange music laced the night air, and woven through the melody was a whispery voice. It was this voice, from an old time, locked in stone, that scraped against the window of Liberty's dreams.

Liberty sat straight up in bed. July groaned and rolled over, then groggily opened one eye. He brushed his hand quickly over his blanket.

What are you doing? Liberty flashed.

Getting the leaves off my covers.

There are no leaves on your covers. But Liberty knew what had happened, for she, too, had been dreaming of dry leaves scraping against a window screen. The Starbuck twins' minds were so attuned to one another that sometimes one twin's dream could spill over like watercolors on paper and run through the channels into the other twin's brain.

Liberty, good grief! Home Run! We've overslept. We'll never make it in time.

July was right, Liberty realized. She had been so caught up in the strangeness of her dreams that she had forgotten why she had awakened. But she knew now that she had awakened because something, some voice, had called. A ray of silver slanted through the skylight. The full moon rode high. They must go now.

July and Liberty climbed through the skylight and down a ladder on the far side of the house, the side away from the bedrooms and nearest the ponies. They led Lightning and Star Eye out of the corral and within seconds were racing for the river. They looked back just once to make sure that no lights had gone on in the house. If they had looked back a second time, they would have seen the figure of a very large wolf. Or was it a wolf? For when it reared up in the darkness, its pointed ears seemed almost to skim the edge of the moon.

14.

Through the Needle's Eye

THE WIND stung their cheeks and the night air had a bitter edge. But the twins rode. They kept to the base of the hogback where the ground was flatter, avoiding the high route up the ridge. They had only one thought: to rescue Home Run.

I think, Liberty flashed as she tried to picture the shape of the mesa on which they had discovered the kiva, *that we should go around the far side of it. Not up the way we went before.*

We shouldn't go up at all, July flashed back. He was riding a few pony lengths ahead, but there was no problem with transmission.

Even in the dead of a moonlit night, the mesa appeared a deep blood red. They had ridden past the path they had first taken to the top and were far into a deeply slashed canyon. Torn and gashed, studded with immense boulders, the terrain seemed frozen in the last writhing posture of some cataclysmic, crunching moment in the earth's history. Gigantic pillars of red rock dwarfed the ponderosa pines and the piñon trees.

July and Liberty slowed the ponies, to look for a clue, any hint of how to get into the kiva where Home Run had fallen and was, they hoped, still alive. The odd rocks with the gaping mouths were piled up in large jumbles as if they had just tumbled from a great height. July shone the flashlight between them to see if any hidden crevice or entryway would be revealed.

The moon, already on the downhill side of the night, began to slide away, but the twins' eyes had grown accustomed to the darkness. *It's almost like this whole side of the mesa just tumbled down.* Liberty looked straight up. Just then July's flashlight illuminated a narrow cleft in the rock.

Here! July teleflashed.

What? Liberty leaned forward in the saddle as July ran his beam of light up and down. *J. B., you gotta be kidding,* she flashed, looking at the small slot in the rock face.

What do you mean, "kidding"? That goes someplace, I can tell. He was out of his saddle and shining the light into the cleft. *It's the beginning of a tunnel or something.*

The cleft was like a V, wider at the top than the bottom, but still not very wide. Using Star Eye for a platform, first July and then Liberty managed to insert themselves through the opening. There was some very fancy body work involved.

My head got through easily, July flashed. *It's my shoulders that are the problem.*

Well, be glad you're not Aunt Honey. That butt of hers would never make it through. A current of giggles burbled through the channels.

Don't make me laugh, Liberty!

After several minutes July realigned his shoulders, making minute turns and adjustments until his shoulders passed through. With July's coaching, it took even less time for Liberty.

Fifteen minutes later the children were walking through a stone corridor. They had gone less than fifty feet when the corridor widened dramatically and they found themselves in a large cavelike room.

July scanned the view overhead. *This could be the place.* He was trying to imagine whether the contours of the ceiling could match the place where he and Liberty had been standing that afternoon when Home Run had vanished. *I'm looking for the smoke hole.*

Don't look any further.

What? You found it, Liberty?

She had not found the smoke hole, but at the edge of the flashlight's beam, she had detected movement. She grabbed the light from July and shone it toward the floor.

And there, within the sacred ceremonial chamber, in the holiest of the holy places, in the sipapu through which the spirits passed, Home Run was busily feeding on what looked like old dried corn kernels.

Home Run! Both twins teleblurted, and raced to the hole. Home Run seemed none the worse for his drop into the kiva. He eagerly drank the water that Liberty poured from her canteen into a small collapsible camping cup.

Ooooh, what are these? Liberty wondered. Mixed in with the corn kernels were the remains of what appeared to have once been bird feathers. *And this corn! It looks absolutely fossilized. Still, I guess it satisfied him.*

It probably is almost a fossil. Remember that part you read about how they used corn and cornmeal as part of the ceremonies, Liberty?

"Well, Home Run," Liberty whispered, "now I guess you can say that this was a lucky breakthrough. I mean, suppose you had fallen into the place where they made arrowheads or something, with no food?"

I don't know, Liberty. The teleflash was cold. *Look over there.* Something in July's tone spilled dread into the channels. Liberty did not want to turn her head, but slowly her eyes followed July's. There was no need for the beam of the flashlight. The skulls gleamed white in the stony darkness.

There were four skeletons. Two were adult-sized, one was the size of a child who was almost a teen, and one, nestled close to one of the adult skeletons, was that of a small baby.

The children walked as if in a trance to the edge of the kiva where the bones lay. The baby's skull lay like a shattered bowl in the dust, the fragments scattered in a semicircle. The other skulls had been crushed.

Finally Liberty managed a sigh.

But I thought these were holy places. There was no human sacrifice in their religion.

This must have been murder. Plain and simple.

Just as July flashed that thought, they heard a scuttling not far off. Home Run was nosing around in a pile of broken pottery, the remains of a basket, and what appeared to be a sandal.

July walked over. *Look, it's their stuff.*

Liberty followed. *Not just their stuff, July!* Her eyes were riveted to a wedge-shaped stone with dried sinew wrapped around it. *The murder weapon!*

She was right. The blade of the large stone ax fitted perfectly the dent in the one skull that was still partly intact. The others were completely shattered.

They thought that perhaps they should have been afraid, but instead Liberty and July felt immeasurably sad. There was a sorrow to the place that clung like mist on a foggy day. It reminded Liberty of the beautiful, desolate music she had dreamed of—the music of Kokopelli, the flute player.

Remember, Liberty? The last carving of the flute player on this very mesa was the one where he was lying on his back.

Yes, I was thinking about that. Maybe that means that this is the place where he finally—rested.

It's like a bad thing did happen here, but I don't think it's a bad place.

Me, neither. It can't be all bad. Good things happened here, too. I just know it.

Liberty's conviction blinked emphatically in the channels. And between the blinks, like the tendrils of a distant melody, they heard the thin hollow sounds of a flute.

They wanted so badly to stay, but they also knew that they must get back before dawn. If it were discovered that they had sneaked out at night, it would be all over. They would never have another chance to return. And they must return to the bloodred mesa—they must. Picking up Home Run, they left quickly, squeezing themselves through the cleft. They found the ponies where they had left them— Star Eye tied to a rock that jutted out next to the cleft, and Lightning, to a nearby juniper. As they pointed the ponies toward home, Liberty looked back over her shoulder.

We'll be back! she flashed, although she did not know exactly to whom she was flashing. Liberty dug her heels into Star Eye's flanks, and she and July raced the dawn home.

15.

A Visit to the SnowFlowers

LIBERTY AND JULY woke up the next morning to a white world. July crawled out of bed to look out the window. The sky was turquoise, the sun was shining, and the slow descent of the falling snowflakes made July feel like he was living in a snow globe. Charly and Molly were already outside building a snowman.

Zanny called up, "You two ever going to get up? What did you do last night to make you sleep this late?"

Zanny's question sent a bolt of fear through Liberty, who had just been on the milky edges of sleep. "Nothing!" she shouted and sat straight up in bed.

Good grief! Liberty, try to look a little more guilty. July tele-flashed a quick warning. *You want to blow the whole thing?*

"Well, hurry up. I've got pancakes cooking down here. And we're supposed to go over to Vera SnowFlower's pueblo. You can see how they do the pottery. Vera is a fantastic little potter."

Liberty and July exchanged disappointed glances. They were determined to get back to the hidden kiva at Blood Mesa, as they now called it. This was going to be tricky. They certainly did not want to arouse suspicion by flatly refusing and saying they had something else to do. Yet they felt a sense of urgency to return there. The music of the flute player had not been a dream. They had both heard it in the telepathic channels. And within the music, there had seemed to be a whisper, like the wind scraping leaves against the adobe. But the words were not yet intelligible.

"So hop to it," Zanny called. "And I'd like you to take your notebooks because I have a nifty idea for a project."

Oh, shoot. The last thing I want to think about is the Southwest curriculum. Why can't she let up and let us be ignorant for a while? July grumbled.

Sometimes it seemed as though Zanny could tune in to the channels. "I know what you're thinking, kids: Oh, gee, why does she have to go and spoil everything with the mention of homework or school? But just remember that it's Friday and if you were home, it would be vocabulary test day. Instead of a vocabulary test we're riding our ponies to a pueblo where for hundreds of years the people have created beautiful pottery with designs handed down from generation to generation."

An hour later the four Starbuck children and Zanny were in the pueblo of Manteca. The snow had stopped. They were standing by a smoldering open fire—burning wood and manure—outside Vera SnowFlower's house. The warm fragrance of baking bread came from a beehive-shaped mud oven, the *horno,* which was built in a corner of the yard. The sun-warmed adobe buildings stacked one upon another seemed to glow against the white landscape.

Vera SnowFlower's mother muttered something in Keresan, the language spoken in Manteca, then turned to the Starbucks and smiled. "Now, for the moment of truth! This is the scary part, when we take the potteries out. Keep your fingers crossed that nothing is broken."

With a pitchfork and a shovel, she began dismantling the fire. First she removed some large, thin slabs of rock. Underneath was a set of old bedsprings. "That's to protect the pottery from the burning cakes of manure, which can cause fire clouds. Vera likes fire clouds on some of her pots, but not today." She poked a tine of the pitchfork into the wire of the bedsprings and began to lift them off.

"Oooooh!" the Starbucks and Zanny exclaimed. On the grate of an old grill, more than a half dozen bronze-colored pots twinkled in the morning sun.

"Not one broken, I think." Grace SnowFlower's voice swelled with pleasure. "Aha, but I do see one little fire cloud, just for Vera, I think."

The children crouched down for a closer look. "What makes it glittery?" July asked.

"That's the mica. You know what mica is? It's that glittery mineral that peels off certain rocks. It gets into the clay around here. That's why we never paint our pots when we use this clay. They are pretty enough without paint. Still, we make beautiful designs. See this one." She put on her gloves and picked up a small, beautifully shaped pitcher. Something quickened in Liberty's and July's minds as the sun glinted off the surface like silver arrows. Embedded on the curving side of the pitcher was a humpbacked figure. It was Kokopelli, and from his flute, like a symbol of the music never heard, a fire cloud rolled.

"Yep, you did a nice job with this one, Vera. Kokopelli is ready to play."

He doesn't look ready to me, Liberty flashed. *He looks trapped.*

That's rude, Liberty, Charly said, tuning in to the channels.

Why don't you just get out of here, Liberty snarled telepathically at her younger sister. *This wasn't an aesthetic judgment. I just said he looked trapped, like you couldn't hear the music.*

Maybe you'd just better leave it at that, Liberty, July interrupted. It was a thinly veiled warning.

I get the feeling that we're being left out of something, Molly chimed in.

Oh, please! Liberty and July telemuttered in unison, then promptly shut down the channels. Molly's and Charly's little snot-glazed noses began to curl into snarls. Under their Davy Crockett caps their brows darkened with their own brand of fire clouds. Liberty couldn't resist.

You both look like a cow pie fell on your faces.

Shut up! they blasted her.

Come on, Liberty, July warned.

There were other pots with embedded figures that Vera and her mother had made. A plate had a lizard on it that looked as if it were crawling right out of the clay, dragging its still-buried tail behind it. There was a pitcher with a bird, its wings spread but not quite flying, and another pot of Vera's, with a running figure.

They all went into Vera's house, where her mother made them hot chocolate. They drank it with warm slices of bread fresh from the *horno.* Vera showed them the room in back where she and her mother worked on their pots when it was too cold out in the yard.

Liberty remembered that Marguerite Greyeyes had said that Vera's rabbit designs were special.

"What's the difference between your rabbits and other potters' rabbits?" she asked.

Vera's mother laughed.

"Show them, Vera. Compare yours to that one of mine over on that shelf."

"See," Vera said. "The ears go back just a bit and so do the feet. Mine are always running. Other potters have theirs standing still or maybe hopping a little bit."

"She's a running girl, our Vera. Maybe she's got some Navajo blood in her. Navajos are good runners. And when Navajo girls get to be thirteen, fourteen years old and have their *kinaaldá*, the ceremony of maturity, they race into the dawn to become strong."

"They do?" Liberty's eyes widened. "How neat!"

"Yep, it's something to do with Changing Woman, the wife of the sun."

Liberty looked over at Vera, who had picked up a small carving tool and was scraping away at another pot with a running figure, this one human. "That looks really good, Vera."

Vera held the small pot away from her and squinted. "Not fast enough," she said, and laughed. "She looks like she's dragging her feet in the clay."

"Vera's a perfectionist," Grace said. "She comes from a long, long line of wonderful potters, going way back many generations on both sides of the family. Vera is going to be much better than me. She has the gifts of her great-great-grandmother Annie Sanchez. Red Corn was her Keresan name, and she was descended from Bear Track."

"No, I'm not that good, Mom," Vera said softly. There was something in her voice that made Liberty think that Vera was just being modest and maybe she did imagine that someday she might be a better potter than her mother. It wasn't a braggy tone. No, it was almost a trace of fear.

16.

Chocolate Blue-Striped Pepper Fish

THAT NIGHT at dinner, Putt was fuming. "Imagine that, will you! I mean the trouble they went to—first the Goodwell Chocolates box. It takes a little doing to find one out here, you know. Those are the most expensive chocolates sold in the whole world. You get them in fancy department stores or shops on Fifth Avenue in New York." He shook his head in disbelief. "To tell you the truth, I was so excited. I mean, I do love chocolates and I have on very rare occasion had one of these fancy Goodwell ones. A big client of Mom's sends them to Starbuck Recital Wear. She usually eats them before she gets them home. So I was practically salivating at the office this afternoon, when suddenly I noticed this strange odor. You know how they package chocolates—so lovely with all those little foil wrappers and then the layer of stiff brown puckered paper . . ." Putnam shut his eyes dreamily behind his thick glasses. "There's always that wonderful tension—first the deciding. Which one to try? Then that marvelous moment of anticipation. Will it be a lemon cream within the dark rich splendor of the chocolate case? Or a rum toffee?"

"Yuck!" Charly and Molly said.

"Or a caramel cordial—oooh, ecstasy—or a praline, double ecstasy! And then the delicious moment of surprise."

"It must have really been a surprise this time," July said.

"The smell was so strong that I took off the first layer of chocolates to see, and there it was—a dead blue-striped pepper fish." Putnam groaned and sank back in his chair by the fire in the kitchen.

"It's so awful," Zanny said. "It's hard to imagine someone going to all that trouble."

"And, of course, where did they get the blue-striped pepper fish? I mean, who knows, maybe they killed it, maybe they decided to martyr it for the cause. After all, the river diversion hasn't even happened yet, so none have died from that. You're right, Zanny, it's a lot of trouble to go to, a terrible waste of energy. And it's disgusting."

"I read this thing online," Charly piped up, "where these bad guys got mad at another bad guy for telling the police about something, and they clonked him on the head and stuffed a dead parakeet in his mouth. Now, that's what I call disgusting."

Putnam blinked and peered at Charly. "Whatever happened to reading *The Bobbsey Twins* or *The Wizard of Oz* or *The Secret Garden*?"

"Oh, Zanny's reading us *The Secret Garden* right now. We read lots of those," Molly said.

Putnam blinked again. "Are you sure it was a parakeet?"

"I think it might have been a canary, Charly," Molly said, wiping her nose on her sleeve.

"That makes more sense," Putnam said. "A canary is sort of a symbol for squealing on someone, or as they say in the criminal world, singing. To sing like a canary is like being a major tattletale."

"Oh," said Charly slowly, "like ratting."

"Oh, my gosh." Molly slapped her cheek. "They could have put a dead rat in his—"

"Don't say it!" Liberty and July screamed.

"Dinner!" Zanny announced.

They all went to bed early. But within minutes of going upstairs, Liberty's and July's hopes of a nighttime foray to Blood Mesa were dashed.

"Look, it's snowing again," Liberty said. "It's so early for snow—barely November."

"It's the high altitude. Dad says that it can snow here as early as September."

"Let's go up on the roof and see what it looks like." They put on their boots, flung blankets around their shoulders, and crawled up the ladder through the skylight. The frigid air felt good. From the high, silent world of the mesa, the stars were points of light amid the immense flakes of falling snow.

Oh, shoot! July telemuttered.

What's the problem? Liberty asked.

There's nothing like a fresh layer of snow to really show them the way, July flashed.

Them. The word lingered in the channels. Somewhere out there they were waiting. The howl of a coyote curled out of the darkness.

Sounds nearby. Liberty shivered.

"'The customary puberty ceremony lasts four days. During this time, the Navajo girl cannot eat sugar or salt.' Molly and Charly would die. 'The young girl is dressed in her best clothes and her hair is tied with a buckskin string.'" The twins could not fall asleep, so Liberty had found a book on Navajo customs and was reading aloud about the *kinaaldá* ceremony that Grace SnowFlower had told them about. "Ooh, listen to this. 'On the morning of the final day following the cornmeal-cake ceremony, the girl lies face down on a pile of blankets and a woman presses her body from head to foot. This is to help shape her body as well as her spirit. Then white clay is applied to her face.' Oooh, cool! 'And then for the third and last time, she races for the dawn.'" Liberty sighed. As coming-of-age ceremonies went, except for the presents, this sounded a lot better than her friend Muriel Braverman's bat mitzvah, which was planned for Muriel's thirteenth birthday. Liberty looked over at July. "You weren't even listening. Doesn't this interest you?"

"What?" July looked up from his book. "Puberty ceremonies for girls—no, not really."

"What's that?" Liberty asked.

"It's all about tracking—pretty interesting. The Navajo were great trackers." July switched to the telepathic channels. *And they were also good at hiding their tracks.*

Even in the snow?

Even in the snow, July flashed crisply. He had read everything he could about tracking. There were the Crazy Eight, the Wolf Pack, the Double and Triple Loop—all patterns designed to confuse and obscure the trail of a horse or a human. There were two entire chapters on the crafty use of plants for disguising one's own trail or following someone else's.

We've got to make ourselves a sagebrush-and-juniper broom to drag behind us. It says here that on hard-packed terrain this is essential.

Liberty crawled to the end of the bed and reached into the niche in the adobe wall where she and July kept the jelly beans. She opened the candy tin and peered in. The supply was getting low. Mostly green ones left. Suddenly Liberty's breath caught in her throat. Fear gushed into the channels.

What is it? July flashed.

Liberty looked up, her face deathly pale, then looked back into the tin. In the corner, next to a green jelly bean, was a small white bead.

A bone bead.

No! July scrambled out of bed and stared into the tin.

A skinwalker's been here, July—a witch, right in our very own bedroom!

Liberty put the lid back on the tin. She was suddenly no longer hungry for jelly beans.

17.

A Hidden Door Gives Way

MARGUERITE GREYEYES had said that a bone bead was like a bad magic spell or a warning. But, spell or warning, it was snow that wiped out any plans to return to Blood Mesa and the hidden kiva. No matter how expert July became at disguising tracks, it would have been useless. The snow turned into a blizzard, and for the better part of a week the high-desert country was buried under a thick covering of white. It was beautiful snow. It never got dirty the way snow did in a city. Putt bought some sleds, and the children spent happy hours sledding down the mesa on which their house perched.

The snow lay over the land like a glistening blanket, muffling sound and decorating the adobe house in a mantle of white frosting, so that it looked like a delicious ginger cake. One white day slipped into the next. Liberty and July never heard nor even thought very often about the whisper in the wind or the strange music of Kokopelli. It all seemed smothered now, lost under the sparkling white of the vast snow blanket.

Finally, when the weather turned warmer, something more than snow seemed to melt. The winter lock on their dreams and fears was released. A box had arrived from Aunt Honey, who had been so busy teaching ice-skating that she'd rarely had time to visit. It was one of the best gifts she had ever given them—a pair of real buckskin moccasins for each of the children and some extra pieces of buckskin for making things. They were winter moccasins that came up to their knees, made for trudging through snow. July was lacing his up and Liberty was tying a buckskin string into her hair when suddenly July flashed, *I think it's time to go.* He didn't have to say where. Liberty knew.

But July, what about the bead, the bone bead?

Forget the bead. It's a cheap rotten trick of a bully, designed to intimidate.

Gads, Liberty thought, July is beginning to sound like Dad—that righteous indignation, the same way Dad had been about the dead fish in the box of chocolates.

But what if we're followed? Liberty asked.

They're not going to follow us. We'll make sure. I know exactly what to do.

You mean the tracking book?

Precisely. We'll spend today making our brushes—they're important—and tomorrow night we'll go. There's no moon

tomorrow. It will be a perfect night. The snow has melted al-
most completely. The river is running with plenty of water, so
we can take our ponies through it for a good distance. They'll
never track us through water, and by tomorrow I will have
mastered the false exits from rivers.

So they went. It was the blackest night imaginable. There was neither moon nor star, for the sky was thick with clouds. But there was a clarity in their minds and a keenness in the channels. They had both studied the tracking book. Liberty, who was so good at keeping whole pictures and patterns in her head, could flash the design of the Double Loop or the Wolf Pack to July, who would figure out just what was needed for the particular terrain. Earlier in the day they had laid a false track with the unwitting help of the little twins, who had been told that they were going to play a new game that was a cross between Simon Says and Follow the Leader. That night, they followed the false tracks, then skillfully disguised the point at which they entered the river. The water was high and sometimes neared the soles of their moccasins. But the ponies did not seem to mind. They made a false exit at the place where they usually crossed for Pink Mesa, and another a good twenty minutes further down the river. Liberty had drawn a map of the terrain from memory. They were sure that if they followed the river this far, they would come out on the other side of the hogback ridge and could head straight for the wash. They carefully erased their tracks with their brooms of sagebrush and juniper.

Don't make it look too even, Liberty flashed as she and July worked. They had covered the soft muddy tracks by filling them in. Now they were sweeping the harder, dry ground of the river.

And pick up any bits that fall off the broom, July added.

Almost two hours later they were standing in the kiva. The skulls were in the same place, as were the murder weapon, the sandals, and the pots. It was all the same. And once again they had heard the music, dim and distant at first, louder when they reached the canyon at the base of the mesa. It was from the odd holes in the rock that the music flowed—slow, hollow, lonely music that had been lost in time and locked in stone for centuries.

Well, here we are, Liberty flashed. She bent over and set down Home Run, who had been nestled in the fleece-lined, stand-up collar of her parka. Liberty and July had felt that it was essential to take the remarkable hamster with them. If he didn't nose things out with all the deliberation of a crack field archaeologist, he crashed into them by accident. Home Run stood still for several seconds and pricked up his ears as if he, too, heard the music.

Naw, impossible. July shook his head.

Don't knock it, Liberty flashed. *Look! He seems to know where he's going and*— Liberty didn't finish the flash. Both twins scrambled after the hamster as he headed for the entrance of the kiva. But instead of turning right and heading down the corridor, Home Run turned left.

Wait a minute, this dead-ends, doesn't it? July flashed.

I thought it did, but look. He's squeezing through that space behind the big rock there.

Liberty, we are not hamsters! There is no way that we're going to get through that one. Look, it even seems like a tight squeeze for Home Run's little butt.

Sure enough, Home Run backed out, but then, undeterred, ran to the top of the boulder to sniff out another opening. July followed and got out his flashlight. Liberty was right behind him. Was it her imagination, or did the music seem louder? Both children suddenly knew that they must get around the boulder, and Home Run himself seemed to be increasingly agitated.

Look! Liberty flashed. In the beam of July's flashlight, she had picked out a familiar pattern—the roughly rectangular shape of . . .

Adobe bricks? she flashed.

July looked up and squinted. *No, I think they're stone but mortared in with adobe. This is a built wall.* He got out his penknife and began to scrape near the bottom of the wall. The dried mud came away easily, revealing between the stones a meshwork of sticks daubed with mud.

In no time July had made a small hole and Home Run dashed through.

But what about us? Liberty sighed.

I'm thinking, I'm thinking. It wouldn't be that hard to make this bigger, but this might be a bearing wall, and it could all come crashing down on top of us.

Couldn't you just make it a little bigger so maybe we could just peek through?

Home Run ran back through the hole, as if to summon the children to follow, and looked up with a most imploring expression on his face.

He might be psychic, but he doesn't have much common sense if he can't see that we won't fit, July telemuttered. But he got down on his knees and began scraping away. Home Run scuttled back through to the other side. July had been scraping for several minutes when his knife, and then his whole hand, went right through.

What happened? Liberty flashed.

I'm not sure. It's as if the wall suddenly thinned out. Let me see. He bent over, wedged the flashlight against the opening, and peered through.

Liberty! This isn't a wall at all. It's a doorway!

18.

A Star Through the Rocks

WITHIN FIVE minutes the twins were on the other side of the door. It had, in fact, been walled up by just a thin layer of mud and sticks. They were now in what looked like a storeroom; it held many large pots, some still partially filled with corn. The music had grown clearer.

July and Liberty followed Home Run out of the room, into another, and down another long corridor. The stonework was beautiful. Walls had been built from rock slabs the size of shoe boxes, each stone carefully dressed or shaped by stone tools. Between them were thinner slabs, layered and stacked, that functioned as the mortar holding the walls together. The false wall of the doorway had been a slapdash job that was totally out of keeping with the beautifully constructed stone walls inside. Many of the walls had collapsed into large piles of rubble as if they had been knocked down by a great force. Home Run scampered straight up a wall; the children followed by climbing up a badly damaged kiva ladder. They were on a large, flat, square space when July felt a wind in his face.

I think we're on a terrace or something.

I see a star! Liberty flashed.

What?

Through that crack in the wall.

But this time it wasn't a wall but rather two huge boulders blocking one side of the terrace. The flashlight battery was wearing down, but the children's eyes had become accustomed to the darkness. Before them loomed two massive gray shapes with black wedges of the night sky cutting into them. In one of these wedges hung a star.

It's the North Star, I'm sure, Liberty flashed. She had a sense of where they stood, now that they had come out from the stone heart of the mesa.

Suddenly there was a polar flash of white light, as if from that very star. The whisper in the wind became a cry, and a bleached shadow swirled up from the wedge between the rocks. It was as if a wisp of the Milky Way had torn loose from the sky.

> *I thought . . . I thought . . .* The whisper in the wind grew into a tremulous voice. *I thought you would never come!* And then laughter like wind chimes broke through the night. *But you have and I am so happy!*

The voice came to them through the telepathic channels. July wondered—but very quietly so as not to interrupt the transmission—if this were the kind of cosmic background radiation that scientists sometimes picked up from deep space, a maverick radio wave. Liberty, however, knew better. This was the whisper embedded in the wind that scraped the leaves against the screen of her bedroom window back in Washington, D.C. This was the whisper wrapped in the melody of the humpbacked flute player's song. This was the ancient voice Liberty had struggled to hear through layers of sleep. It wasn't saying "cue-me" at all. Not "come to me." No, it was a name: *Kyumi.* The name twinkled in the channels like a small galaxy.

> *And there is my pot and you have opened the door to my bones.*

The twins could hear the chimes in the wind as Kyumi laughed, but they still could not quite see her. She was a bright smear in the night.

In one of the three walls, there was a niche like the ones in the children's bedroom, and in this niche there were pieces of a broken pot. Home Run was nosing at more fragments on the floor below. The curve of one side of the pot remained, enough to give Liberty and July a clear idea of its shape. But what became even more clear as the twins studied the fine painted lines was that this, in fact, was the work of the left-handed potter, the master potter. The words of Marguerite Greyeyes came back to them. "Pieces like these can still have the spirit in them, and some believe that if you listen carefully enough you can hear, like a faint voice, the spirit songs of the wind."

Gently and with great reverence the children gathered up the pieces. Although these were not religious relics, they were sacred in a special human way. Liberty opened her parka and took the wool scarf from her neck, and carefully they put the pieces in the scarf. When there was no more room, July took off his flannel shirt and used it, shivering under his parka. With each fragment they gently placed in the shirt and the scarf, they sensed that something was taking shape and becoming whole. And when they put the last piece in July's shirt, there stood before them a girl in white buckskin. She looked not more than a year or two older than they were.

She was still transparent. They could see the stars through her fringed dress, and the boulder through her jet-black hair. She began to speak.

My story is a long one. I can only begin it tonight. You must come back again to hear the end, and then you must help me . . . please.

Oh yes, oh yes! The twins flashed in unison. All the sadness that loomed throughout the kiva seemed to swell now like a sob in the back of their throats.

*My name is Kyumi. I am of the Sweet Water Clan.
It was here on this plaza that I was murdered six
hundred years ago.*

The children gasped. It was several seconds before they
could even think. Finally July spoke.

Yes, we found the ax.

> *You found the ax, but more important, you found
> parts of my pot—my last pot—the one that every
> master potter should be buried with.* There was an
> urgency in her voice. *You must take all these pieces
> back to the kiva and put them with my bones. This
> is most important.*

Kyumi flickered like the flame of a candle at the top of
the kiva ladder they had climbed to the terrace. They followed her unquestioningly.

A few minutes later they had placed the pot shards by
the bones. There was a deep sigh.

> *No, it is not the bones sighing. It's me.*

Kyumi shimmered near the sipapu. She indeed could
have been one of the ancient Air Spirits from the beginning
of time, Liberty thought.

Kyumi spoke. *The bones are mere clothes, cast-off clothes. They do not matter in themselves, just like the pottery fragments are cast off from the shape— separately they are meaningless but together they clothe the spirit of the pot. My spirit has never rested. It is caught between the spirit land and the land of the living, wandering the earth, trying to find a place to go.*

Just like the story, July and Liberty said at once.

Ahh, yes. Kyumi's laugh was bitter now. *Like the story told about Coyote, who made the whirlwind come and slam the door on the place for spirits. But it was not Coyote who did this to me. It was evil men, dressed in skins of bears and wolves, who murdered me.*

Skinwalkers! Liberty gasped, thinking of the bone bead she had found in the jelly-bean tin.

My grandfather and my mother can rest in peace and not wander, because their work was completed. The baby was too young to have work and she died in her mother's arms. So her circle of peace is complete. But I was in the midst of the first part of my life as a master potter—and I was murdered on the terrace just as I had put the finished pot in the niche. My bones were taken here, away from my last pot. Over the centuries, the earth shifted, the pot cracked, some shards fell from the terrace to the ground below, to the river . . .

River? July exclaimed.

Yes, six hundred years ago the river flowed differently from the course it now follows. Kyumi paused. *Several pieces of my last pot are missing, carried away by the river or fallen through cracks in the earth. The earth shifts, the mountains and rivers move, the pot shards become buried or lost, but I need them.* Her voice broke. *I need them. Only then can I rest in peace. Only then will the spirit of my work and my being join the circle of peace like that of my baby sister, who sleeps with our mother's spirit. Help me, twins! Please help me!*

19.

The Southwest Curriculum Kicks Butt!

LIBERTY AND JULY slipped into the house on the mesa just before dawn. They were so excited that, tired as they were, sleep was impossible.

"We have to find those missing pieces."

"But, July, how do we begin to look? Especially when there was an earthquake. I think that's what she meant."

"That's exactly what she meant. And although it might have shattered the pot, in another way it helped."

"How do you mean?"

"It's fairly simple. Look, Liberty, basically we've discovered a lost cliff dwelling. The reason it has never been discovered is because all those rocks tumbled down during the earthquake and shut off that whole end of the canyon. Locked it behind huge stone boulders just like the ones that were on the terrace where Kyumi appeared. Now, if it hadn't been hidden, you can bet pothunters would have been in there years ago and taken everything, including the pot in the niche and all the pieces that fell on the floor."

"You're right, July. But some of those pieces dropped into where the river once flowed and were carried away."

"Precisely. Like the two that Home Run found when we were at Pink Mesa. And they were stolen."

"I am sure that the two stolen pieces were from Kyumi's pot," Liberty said emphatically. "I remember their shapes and the designs. I can just imagine them fitting in perfectly with the fragments that we picked up on the terrace. I know it."

"That might mean that the thieves have some other pieces of this pot, too," July said.

"Why's that?"

"Well, remember how Marguerite Greyeyes said those fragments were of absolutely no value by themselves, since the thieves would not have known where they came from?"

Unless. Both twins switched simultaneously to the channels, for the thought was so powerful that they could not speak it aloud.

Unless, Liberty continued, *they did know where the pieces had come from.*

Or unless they had already found others in another place. A place where the old river used to flow.

Where would that be?

I don't know, but I bet I know who does.

Who?

Dad.

Putnam was thrilled at the twins' new enthusiasm for geography; Zanny did such a wonderful job with these curriculums she thought up. Yes, indeed, he told them, the course of the Spirit River had changed over the centuries. In fact, the diversion project would take the river much closer to its original path. He showed them half a dozen maps indicating the river's present position and where it had been. When the children asked to borrow the maps to study further, Putnam agreed enthusiastically. He would never be one to stand in the way of the intellectual development of his own children.

You see! July exclaimed telepathically. *Here's Blood Mesa right here on this topographical map that shows where the river used to flow. Look, it was actually the canyon it flowed through. And guess what the canyon is called?*

What?

The Canyon of Lost Souls! Is that strange or what!

Look what else. Liberty's finger traced the river's old course. *It used to swing in right next to Pink Mesa—where we found the two pieces. The water must have carried them there. But we really didn't look anyplace else except Pink Mesa. There could be other places along this bend of the old river where some more fragments might have been carried.*

But Liberty, it's like looking for a needle in a haystack.

Not with Home Run it isn't.

But even Home Run could use a little help now and then. And the one person who could give it to him was Kyumi.

Before they started a search, Liberty and July knew they must go back to the hidden kiva in the lost city on Blood Mesa. Zanny was taking the little twins over to Manteca that day for more pottery lessons with Vera SnowFlower. Liberty and July begged off, saying they were doing a major geography project in which they planned to make an exact-scale three-dimensional model showing the dramatic shift in the landscape of this region of New Mexico. They asked their father, who had to go into Albuquerque, to pick up a five-pound bag of instant papier-mâché and some poster paints.

"Yeah, and some chipboard, or something, for the base," July added.

Putt was beaming. "I think it's just wonderful how this Southwest curriculum is kicking in!"

It's kicking butt is what it's doing! July flashed.

20.

Kyumi's Story

so, you see, they tried to make it appear that my grandfather and my mother and I were practicing witchcraft, Kyumi explained.

So that's the meaning of the owl feathers? Liberty asked. *I wondered about them when we first found Home Run here.* She picked up the raggedy remnant of one of the feathers.

Yes.

And they had to murder you for that? It was a setup, July said angrily.

We weren't witches, Kyumi said. *But the feathers of an owl were taboo. They were thought to be the tools of witches. And the witches did not work for the harmony of the people.*

But why did they do it?

They did it because the times were hard. It brings out the bitterness in people. The dryness had been on the land for almost five harvests. Our people, the people of these dwellings, were better off than many in other tyukis. *Our land was more fertile. We had more food stored so our baskets of beans and corn were not as low. But we, too, were beginning to starve. Hunger causes a meanness of the spirit. There were grumblings.*

   There was one man who was hungry not just for food, but for power. His name was Lopki. There were many disagreements. My grandfather, one of the elders of the council, felt we should allow some of the people from a settlement down the river to join us. We had more. We should share. It is true that my grandfather had a son who had married into that tribe. So maybe this was part of his reasoning. Many people objected. Lopki saw this as a chance. He began the witchcraft rumors.

He planted the feathers? July asked.

Yes. Then during the moon of the Sky Spider, when the men go out to the fields to prepare to dance for the rains, and the women and the old people stay behind until the dawn, that is when he did it. It was Lopki and his friend who came dressed in the skins of wolves.

And murdered you.

All of us. First me, on the terrace, just as I had put my pot up. There was no one around. Then my grandfather, mother, and baby sister as they slept. He waited for my father on his way home from the fields. You see, my father would have been expecting to pass me in the dawn. For I was a yolla *maiden.*

A "yolla maiden"?

I was a moon short of my fourteenth birthday— almost a woman—a yolla *maiden. And there is a special ceremony. Oh, how long I had waited to be a* yolla *maiden and run east toward the rising sun. My best friend had done it the year before. I would get to run with my favorite cousin. And I was such a good runner. I knew that I could have broken the mesa before the sun turned it rose.*

Pink Mesa! The children exclaimed excitedly. They looked at their map. It must be the same mesa.

> *Yes, that is it,* Kyumi said, not even looking at the map.

But it's never pink, Liberty said.

> *Oh, you must be there at dawn, at the precise minute the sun slips over the horizon. Before that, the top glistens like a golden thread against the sky. That is the challenge.* Kyumi's voice swelled with excitement. *To break the golden thread before the sun does and turns the mesa rose. That is why we call it breaking the mesa.*

She sighed and the sigh seemed to swell and fill the kiva. Liberty felt something deep within her stir as she grasped the horrible meaning of a life cut short. This was the truth of it—all the races Kyumi had never run, the promises shattered like pottery, the dreams snatched away.

July was thinking about the course of the river and the course of the race. *You had to cross the river then during the race to Pink Mesa?*

> *Yes. But it was shallow, especially at the time of the Spider Moon.*

We found the two pottery fragments that we told you about, the ones we think came from your last pot, on Pink Mesa, but we couldn't find any more.

> *You found them on that side of the river?* Kyumi seemed surprised. *I would think that you would have found them on this side. There was a bend where everything seemed to catch, where the current ran slower. There were some caves in the rocks there.*

There were? both twins exclaimed.

> *Oh, yes. They were favorite caches for hunters going out. And the rock there was good for flint knapping—making arrowheads and chisels and axes.*

No kidding, Liberty said. *I wonder if there would still be anything left.*

> *Follow me,* Kyumi said. *I cannot leave this mesa, but at least now I can wander the ruin that was my home. And I can show you the signs of flint knapping—what the stone chips look like. So you can look for this place near the caves where the flint knappers worked.*

They followed her out of the kiva, through a long corridor, and up and across terraces.

Why couldn't you leave the kiva before? July asked.

> *Because of the wall that Lopki built where the door once was, before you opened it again. According to our customs, when a person dies, a hole is made in the back of their house for the spirit to leave through so they can join the others in the spirit world. But when a witch dies, the spirit must be sealed away forever or else trouble is caused. That is why Lopki filled in the doorway—so our "evil" spirits would not wander the earth, making trouble. When you opened the door I could go to where you found me—near the fragments of my last pot on the terrace.*

So aren't you free to go to the spirit world now?

> *Ah!* Kyumi paused as they moved onto another terrace. She raised one finger in the air, but it seemed to dissolve in a shaft of sunlight that fell through an opening in the boulders blocking the front of the terrace. *If you find all the pieces of my pot and bring them to me, then I can leave and join my family in the land of the spirits—but only then.*

Something quickened in the hearts of the Starbuck twins.

See, on the ground here? said Kyumi. *This was the flint-knappers' terrace.*

The ground was strewn with small, thin flakes of pinkish stone. As July bent over to pick some up, Liberty looked out through the wide opening between the boulders. This part of the cliff dwelling was very high up and she could see the immense clouds, like ramparts against the brilliant turquoise sky. She went to the edge and wedged her foot in a niche, to hoist herself up for a better view of the deep canyon below. Liberty gasped. A rainbow-shaped bridge was flung across the entire span of the rock canyon. The mountains beyond appeared dim and blue in the distance. Liberty had never seen such natural beauty.

Yes, Kyumi was saying, *the flint-knappers' terrace was a special place. It had to be high and a bit away from the people below.* She laughed. *When a man was chipping out an arrow or lance point and broke it after hours of work, he would get very angry and throw his mistakes over the edge. It would not have been a good place to live, right below the flint-knappers' terrace. You would always be getting hit on the head with mistakes.*

July and Liberty knew that they must leave if they wanted to have time to search for the flint-knappers' spot and the caves near Pink Mesa. So they promised Kyumi that they would come back the next day, and they hoped that they would be returning with the pottery.

Shoot! Double shoot! July telepathically fumed. The twins were crouched behind a chamisa bush hidden in the deep shadows of an overhanging cliff. July folded up his collapsible telescope.

They're over there, at least five of them.

Are they Indians?

I don't know. I can't tell from here. They have a couple of horses, though.

And then as bright as a polished bone bead the idea glimmered in the channels.

Pothunters!

The ones who stole the fragments? Are they looking for more?

Liberty and July crouched down on the ground behind the chamisa bush. They would not move until the five figures went away. If these were pothunters, they were not mere thieves; they trafficked not just in stolen artifacts, but instilled terror as well. The twins remembered the fear in Marguerite's eye; Liberty recalled the dark feeling she'd had deep inside when she discovered the bead in the jelly-bean tin.

The children shrank back into the lengthening afternoon shadows and quickly gave up the idea of looking that day.

"I'll say this," July said later, looking at the ground as they came into the final stretch before the house on the mesa. "These people don't take any trouble at all to cover their tracks."

"July, you're really getting good at this. How can you tell the tracks are theirs?"

"One of their horses has shoes and one doesn't. And they are horses, not ponies like ours. You can tell because their hooves are bigger."

Liberty studied the hoof marks for a few minutes. It didn't take her long to pick up the rhythm of the horses' stride. She also began to detect a boot print along the trail.

"They sure did take a route close to our house," she muttered.

The tracks became obscured at the part of the trail that turned into the old dirt road. At least three cars or trucks appeared to have passed by that day already, in addition to the tracks that Putnam had made when he had left for Albuquerque.

July and Liberty had drunk a quart of milk and moved through two baloney sandwiches and a bag of tortilla chips before they noticed Zanny's note.

Dear L & J:

    *Ride over to Vera SnowFlower's pueblo. We'll still
be there and you can help with pottery and maybe
make some yourself. And by the way, I have a great
surprise for you that I think you'll love.*

                Cheers,
                Zanny,
                your ever-lovin' nanny

21.

Some Surprise

LIBERTY AND JULY were riding behind and fuming.

Some surprise!

Just what we always wanted to do—go to Rancho Eleganza and spend two days taking mud baths, having facials, and seeing Aunt Honey ice dance in one of her dumb outfits. I cannot believe this. How will we ever find the lost fragments? And Zanny? How can she do this? Aunt Honey drives her nuts. But here she is, ready to sell out for mud baths and beauty treatments. That is not what I call moral fiber!

It had been fun at Vera's up until the news of the surprise. They had all made small pots, building them slowly and carefully out of neatly rolled coils. Vera said they should come back soon so she could teach them how to polish the pots.

Vera SnowFlower now stood in the doorway of her family's adobe home, waving and watching the Starbucks and Zanny wind down the steep trail. She liked being with them, even though she couldn't tell the little twins apart. But suddenly Vera blinked. She felt her heart jump like a desert toad escaping a rattlesnake. Out from under the saddle blankets of Liberty and July Starbuck had floated two dark feathers. Vera waited until the ponies had gone around the bend, then raced to where the feathers had fallen.

She stood very still and looked down. "No!" Owl feathers! She dared not speak the words aloud. What people had been saying must be true! She had heard the rumors about the father, but nobody had seen the owl feathers in his car. Her mother had said that it was all just gossip. Marguerite Greyeyes had become very angry. And the whole notion of witches and owl feathers was stupid, Vera's own mother had told her. But even as her mother had spoken, Vera had noticed a nervous flicker behind her mother's eyes. She stared down at the owl feathers quivering in the wind. She could see the downy underside. This wasn't a rumor. This was real. Her heart turned cold as if something within her had died. She had thought, after all, that the Starbuck children were friends.

22.

Runny Noses on Ice

"COULDN'T YOU just eat them up!" the tall lady with the black lacquered hair cooed.

Oh, yeah! Snot and all, Liberty flashed to her brother.

The older twins and Zanny were standing at the edge of the ice-skating rink at Rancho Eleganza with Roz, the owner and Aunt Honey's college chum. Aunt Honey, Charly, and Molly were spinning around on the ice, doing a routine called Satin Baby Dolls that Aunt Honey had taught all the children years ago. Liberty and July had refused to do it since third grade. Even Charly and Molly had said a flat no to the baby-doll outfits of pink bloomers, pinafores, bonnets, and prop baby bottles. They insisted instead on a junior version of Aunt Honey's outfit, which was part of the Starbuck Recital Wear line and consisted of gold satin tuxedo cutaway jackets with sequined lapels, gold leotards, and glittery top hats.

The brilliance of the costumes alone nearly eclipsed the stars as Aunt Honey and the little twins spun, glided, and jumped across the ice accompanied by the *ooohs* and *aaaahs* of the spa guests.

"Aren't they adorable?" gushed one guest as the two little girls launched a series of bunny hops that made their top hats bobble about.

"Fetching, absolutely fetching," said another.

"And look at Honey!" Aunt Honey had just gone into a sit-spin, then a spiral, and was now exploding in a series of back toe-jumps. Her eyes flashed behind thick globs of mascara, while her brass-colored hair never budged a millimeter.

The whole thing is enough to make you throw up, July telemuttered.

Molly skated by fast, did a quick hockey stop, turned, and flashed to her brother, *They love us, poop head!*

Oh, stuff it, twerp! Liberty flashed.

You're just jealous. Charly sculled by backward and stuck her tongue out at her older brother and sister.

The music was building to a crescendo and Aunt Honey was going into a fit of jumps, loops, spins, and spirals. The little twins raced around her, doing bunny hops and spins, like gold moons in a frenetic orbit around a manic sun.

They had been at the spa for just a few hours, but Liberty and July were growing increasingly depressed and hopeless. This was the last place on earth they wanted to be. How could they ever help Kyumi from here? How could they ever find the pottery fragments from here, at Rancho Eleganza, where a lot of chubby, neurotic ladies spent thousands of dollars to get massaged, pummeled, and steamed into shape? The twins had soon become bored on the exercise machines. The whirlpool and the swimming pool were fun, but a person couldn't stay in long—they had started to shrivel in the whirlpool after ten minutes. Zanny, on the other hand, was having the time of her life. There would be hardly enough time to fit in all the beauty treatments that she wanted to pursue—the salt glow, the aromatherapy facial, the dry sauna, the wet sauna, the East Indian cleansing treatment, not to mention the famous mud baths.

July and Liberty went to bed, in their luxurious private rooms, feeling distraught. The older twins' bedrooms were connected by a short corridor that did not seem to impede communication. They each looked out their window toward the dark profiles of the mountains. Unlike the jagged, rugged mountains of the north, these mountains rose in gentle rhythmic waves. They reminded Liberty of large sleeping women.

Liberty, we are surrounded by large sleeping women, July flashed. *That's what this place is about.*

Liberty giggled but she did not feel very happy inside. She was thinking about the hidden kiva and the circle of peace that the bones of Kyumi's mother and baby sister slept in. Outside that circle, everything seemed shattered, as incapable of holding peace as a broken vessel is of holding water.

She didn't like the feel of Rancho Eleganza, either. There were pictures of coyotes all over, even on the plates and napkins, the towels and the sheets. They had coyote sweatshirts in pink or turquoise for sale in the gift shop.

There was a lot of art at the spa. Aunt Honey had said that Roz was a major collector and had one of the finest collections of Southwestern and Native American art in the world. Roz was very rich; her father had been a Texas oil billionaire. She seemed nice enough, though, Liberty thought.

Just enough, July flashed.

What do you mean—enough what?

What you were just thinking—she's barely nice enough.

July was right, Liberty realized. Roz probably was one of those people who was simply not at ease with children.

She treats kids as pets. I can spot that type a mile away, July flashed. *That's why she was cooing over Charly and Molly whizzing around in those little gold tuxedos on their ice skates.*

She might be into kids as pets but she's not into pets as pets. She'd have a major fit if she knew Home Run was here, Liberty answered.

The twins didn't even want to imagine what Roz would do if she found out that Liberty and July had sneaked a rodent into Rancho Eleganza.

Probably wrap the poor little critter in herbs and serve him up as a low-cal snack.

July! That's horrendous. Don't even think it. Zanny had wanted to put Home Run in his cage with plenty of food and leave him in the barn. She had given a brief lecture on the thermal capacities of horse manure. But Molly and Charly nearly had heart attacks when they thought of their dear little Home Run packed in horse doo doo. The Starbuck children had decided they just couldn't do it and sneaked Home Run off to Rancho Eleganza.

I don't understand why Dad had to go to Albuquerque for three whole days. If he hadn't, we wouldn't have to be here.

I know, but there's no use thinking about that. We're Powerless, Liberty, July said, his telepathic voice drenched in resignation. *That's a kid's fate in life—everyone else makes the decisions and bosses you around.*

Liberty hated the notion of being powerless. It bugged the heck out of her. She thought of Kyumi and the race she had almost run into the dawn. Nobody could boss you around after that! After you had—what had Kyumi called it?—broken the mesa.

Liberty could tell that July was asleep. There was a stillness in the channels. She scrunched down under the blankets and stared out the window at the mountains that slept like immense women under the dome of the starry night.

A half hour later she was still staring out the window. She simply could not sleep. Finally she got up and pulled out the book her mother had been reading to them when they first arrived in New Mexico.

She reread the story about Turkey. Liberty liked reading about underdogs—or underturkeys, in this case. Everybody had been so quick to get mad at Turkey for bringing nothing, yet he had brought the most important thing of all—the seeds to grow food. She giggled as she felt Home Run's fur tickling her toes. She lifted the sheet and called to him, "Come on, Home Run. Come up here—I'll read you a story."

With the hamster nestled in the bunched-up flannel of her nightgown, Liberty began to read a tale she had never read before. "How could I have missed this one, Home Run?" she wondered aloud. "'The story of the Hero Twins, Monster Slayer and Born of Water.'" She turned to the first page. "'In the beginning there was Changing Woman and her two children, who were twins and were thirteen years old . . .' What do you know, Home Run, twins and just our age."

The short story told how the villages of the Anasazi people were plagued by terrible monsters. The twins visited their father, the sun, and stole from him lightning and magic weapons with which they destroyed the monsters. Liberty sighed as she read the last line. "Well, those kids sure as heck were powerful, even if it is just a story."

23.

In the Coyote's Den

"LOOK AT this, July!" Liberty was studying a brochure of Rancho Eleganza just before they were all to join Roz for an early dinner in her private dining room.

"What?"

"Look at this picture." She pointed at a color photo of a beautiful rock bridge that spanned a canyon. Its red rock soared into the turquoise sky like a bow. *It's the rock rainbow we saw from the flint-knappers' terrace.*

You're right! It's the exact same one. Let me read this. July snatched the brochure. *Liberty, do you realize what this means?*

Of course.

We're much closer to the ruins than we thought.

In the brochure, they call this "a strenuous hike for experienced hikers." Translate that as miserable for fat folks out of shape.

But that's not us!

The knowledge that they were closer to the kiva than they had thought made July and Liberty infinitely happier. There might be a way they could get back to Kyumi within the next three days, or however long it would be until their dad returned from Albuquerque and Zanny got bored with herbal baths.

Then things happened fast.

Aunt Honey insisted that the invitation to dine with Roz in her private quarters was very special, an honor equivalent to being invited to dine at the captain's table on a luxury ocean liner. This meant nothing to the twins, since they had never been on a luxury liner.

"Remember, kids," Zanny said as they all spruced up for dinner. "Party manners."

"Come on, Zanny!" July said.

"Well, I know that you two know how to behave—but, Charly and Molly, no bathroom jokes, please. And here." She took two little hankies out of her pocket and gave one to each twin. "Please use these and don't wipe your noses on your sleeves."

"Remember when they used the tablecloths at Muriel Braverman's brother's bar mitzvah?" Liberty said.

"Oh, how gross." Zanny wrinkled her nose.

"Shut up, Liberty," Charly snarled.

"Okay, are we all ready? And remember, if we're really nice, I think she'll let us take those special mud baths. She said we could have our turn when this week's spa guests left and before the new group arrived."

It just might be fun, Liberty thought. The idea of squishing down into the mud was appealing.

Do you believe what we're looking at? Liberty flashed.

No! July was aghast.

What is it? Molly and Charly asked. There was no way that Liberty and July would be able to keep this from the little twins. The best they could hope for would be to keep it from Zanny until the time was right. And since Zanny could not enter into the telepathic channels, that would be easy. All of them, including Aunt Honey, were sitting in Roz's dining kiva, as Roz called it, eating off specially commissioned pottery plates with designs of petroglyphs around the rims. Niches in the walls held beautiful objects and Indian artifacts. And in one large square niche was a display of ancient pottery—some broken, others pieced together.

Remember when we found the fragments from the old pot? July flashed.

The ones that were stolen? Molly asked.

Precisely, Liberty said.

Yeah, so? flashed Charly.

The pot those pieces came from is right over there on that shelf in the niche. Then Liberty flashed a stern warning. *Be careful, Molly and Charly. Don't both stare at once. She's watching us.*

"You're admiring my pottery, Liberty?" Roz said slowly, her voice dropping to a husky whisper.

"Oh, yeah." Liberty desperately tried to sound casual.

"It's all museum quality," Roz said. Honey nodded and smiled, clearly impressed by her ritzy friend. But Zanny gave a tight, barely polite grimace.

All for a mud bath, Liberty silently fumed.

"You have an appreciation for pottery?" One thin arched eyebrow climbed toward Roz's hairline, but her lizardlike eyelids, half closed and painted a greenish gold, did not move.

Liberty felt terribly uneasy, as if she were on the verge of being sneered at. Or was it something worse? She could not appear to know too much or she would arouse suspicion.

July attempted to help Liberty out. "We were just over at Manteca and we were learning how to make pots from this little girl over there, Vera SnowFlower."

"Oh yes . . . The SnowFlowers are a well-known pottery family. They go quite far back in time—an old line of great potters. I am sure your little friend is quite wonderful."

Oh, I just hate the way she says "little friend"! Liberty telemoaned.

Liberty, Liberty, Charly and Molly were flashing madly. *Are you sure this is the same pot? Do you think she's the one who stole the pieces?*

It is the same pot, kids, but I would think if she had the stolen pieces she would have put them on the shelf and patched them into the pot. But, Charly and Molly, you can't let on that you know anything.

I wonder if she'd let us take a closer look, Molly said.

Don't ask! flashed Liberty.

Wait a second, July flashed back. *It's not a bad idea. They're so little. Remember what we were saying—that she thinks of them like little pets.*

She does? Charly and Molly both said. *What do you mean by that?*

Never mind. July's right. Ask, with all your sweetness and innocence, if you can take a closer look. July and I will pretend to look bored.

Roz seemed more than happy to show off her collection. "Oh, yes, of course. But remember, no touching!" Roz raised one very long painted fingernail, which was about twice as long as a press-on nail. But it was not her nails that caught Liberty's attention. She could see now that Roz's eyes were glittering slits of green, just like the emerald eyes of the coyote pin on the scarf wrapped around her throat.

"Admiring my pin, are you, Liberty?"

Liberty nearly jumped out of her skin. This woman had eyes in the back of her head, and everywhere else, too. She had all the keenness of a stalking animal.

Pull yourself together, Liberty. You're not concentrating. July was right. She was letting Roz get under her skin.

Listen, July was flashing. *It looks to me like a lot of that pot is here, and when you put that with what we found in the ruins, there might only be a few pieces missing—like two!*

What ruins? Charly flashed.

We'll explain more later.

There was a sudden, blaring flash from Charly.

Home Run's been here! The message illuminated the channels.

What? Liberty and July both flashed.

His poop is right here on the shelf, behind that second pot from the end. I'd recognize it anyplace.

Obviously he's discovered this stuff before we did. But hush. Look interested in what Roz is saying, Liberty ordered.

"Mud baths? Oh, yes." They were all agreeing cheerfully. "We'd love it."

"Well, they totally relax you and make you very sleepy. Oh, and Zanny, I'll give you an aromatherapy facial—it's heaven on earth." Roz sighed. "As a matter of fact, I think it would do wonders for you children, too."

"Oh, Roz, you're just too kind!" Honey gushed.

"Not at all, dear." She spoke softly, but as she looked directly at Liberty, her green eyes were as hard as emeralds.

24.

Mud!

THERE WAS barely enough time to tell Charly and Molly the whole story. In fact, they did not tell them everything because it was too complicated to explain Kyumi. Kyumi was, after all, a ghost, and they were afraid that the little kids might be frightened of her. So Liberty and July simply said that the pot was very important to its rightful owner.

You mean like their life depends on it?

Well, not their life exactly. More like their— July groped for the right word.

Spirit, Liberty flashed.

There was a knock on the door.

"Kiddos!" It was Aunt Honey. "Come on, you'll be late for the mud baths. They're so relaxing. You should see Zanny."

The therapy room was a faithful replica of a kiva, but instead of a sipapu and a smoke hole, there were several sunken bathtubs and a skylight. The baths were filled with mud. The only light besides the moon and the stars coming through the skylight overhead was that of scented candles. Soft music played. Zanny was wrapped up like a mummy and lying on a slab.

"Oh, it's wonderful, kids," she said groggily.

"What did they do to her, Aunt Honey?" Molly asked.

"Oh, that's the mud wrap. They shovel hot mud on top of you and wrap you up like a mummy. It's very relaxing."

But the little twins didn't think so.

Are they going to bake her? Molly telewhimpered. For indeed she looked like something rolled up in dough.

This place is creepy, Charly flashed.

It is, kids, but keep calm. Stay alert, July added.

"Oh, children," Aunt Honey was saying, "you don't have to be wrapped up if you don't want."

"Yeah, I think we'll just stick to the mud baths," said July.

"That's fine," said Roz sweetly. "I have a special, very relaxing blend of mud that will be perfect for your young energetic bodies."

Watch it, Liberty flashed as the children slipped off the robes they were wearing over their bathing suits. They climbed into one large tub that could hold them all. Aunt Honey was in a smaller tub beside them.

"Ooooh!"

"Mmmm."

It did feel wonderful.

"Isn't this heaven?" Aunt Honey sighed and leaned her head back on a pillow attached to the side of the tub.

Mud, glorious mud. Don't fight it; it's so wonderful! Liberty and July felt themselves sinking, sinking, sinking away into the warm muddy nothingness.

Charly and Molly, however, were feeling anything but relaxed. They felt jumpy inside, as though a bunch of toads were hippety-hopping around.

She's put something in this mud, Charly flashed. *It's making everyone else go to sleep, but I feel ready to jump out of my skin.*

Me, too.

Look, even Aunt Honey! She's snoring . . .

Here comes Roz. Maybe we should pretend we're asleep, too.

"I think everyone is sleeping like babies. That mixture really is relaxing." It was Roz's voice.

"Should hold them till morning," another voice said. "Give us plenty of time to unload the shipment."

"Now, when are our friends due?"

"An hour or so."

"We are going to be tough bargainers this time."

Molly, what's going on?

I don't know, but if we pretend that we're asleep, we might find out.

Do you think we can ever wake up Liberty and July? It seems real important that they get that pot to the person.

I don't know. Hold on. Here they come. I think they're going to move us.

A few minutes later, all the Starbuck children, Aunt Honey, and Zanny had been transported back to their bedrooms and put into their beds, which had been covered with rubber sheets to protect the regular sheets from the mud. This was all part of the usual mud-bath therapy, but Charly and Molly were right. An extra dose of a powerful desert plant had been added to the muddy brew, normally relaxing enough to induce a torpor by itself. However, very young bodies often react differently to medicines, natural herbs, or chemicals than older bodies do. The two littlest Starbucks had never felt more alert—or, for that matter, more panicked—in their lives.

How are we going to wake them up? the little twins flashed through the corridor to each other. Charly stood looking at the muddy lump that was Liberty as Molly looked at July. Fear welled up in their throats. This was not the way it was supposed to be. Liberty and July were the ones who always figured things out and bossed them around. No matter how many bad, mean things Charly and Molly had ever said about their sister and brother, they had always, deep down, trusted them. This was really scary. But then they remembered something that gave them a grain of courage.

We're turkeys—we're hero turkeys. And they thought of

the story Zanny had told them about how it was Turkey, the most unlikely of all the animals, who brought the important seeds to the new Fifth World.

We'd better start cleaning them up. Charly looked down at Liberty and went to get a washcloth.

Liberty was dreaming of a dark, dark place—a place of ooze and warm mud and slime, a place at the beginning of time, a place inhabited by worms and slugs, where things crept and slithered and not even the insects had wings. It was the Black World, that first world. But something was pushing her, pushing and pressing and kneading her, even shoving her. Was she slithering toward a hole, a passageway? Was there a thin crack of blue light ahead? Was she dreaming or waking? She felt herself being pinched; she felt fingers molding her body. Was she a young maiden being shaped and molded for her *kinaaldá* ceremony?

"Ouch!"

"Sssh!" Charly hissed. *The press-on nails work. One quick little jab right in the armpit,* she flashed to Molly in July's room.

In another minute July, too, was awake and Charly and Molly had told their older brother and sister what they had overheard in the mud room.

So they think we're sleeping soundly, July flashed.

Yep, the little twins answered.

Well, let's see what's going on with this shipment. Through the window, July noticed the lights of a pickup truck as it pulled in.

We need just one person to go out and eavesdrop. July said. *We might make too much noise if it's all of us, and they might even send someone back to check on us.*

It was decided that Liberty should be the one to go. So she crept through the halls toward Roz's office, which in the split-level building was a half floor below the level with the bedrooms and the dining room.

Suddenly Liberty heard distinct voices. She stopped, hardly daring to breath. It sounded as though the voices were coming up through the tile. Then Liberty spotted a heating vent on the floor. It went directly through to Roz's office.

"What do you mean you didn't bring those last two fragments? Isn't that what this whole negotiation has been about?" Roz's voice was a thin hiss. It slithered, hot and venomous, up through the air vent. Liberty's heart beat thunderously in her chest. She was sure that the cold tile floor would transmit its raucous, pulsating rhythm. Keep calm, she ordered, and then flattened herself against the floor. She must hear more.

"We're keeping our options open," someone said coolly.

"What options?" Roz said in a scalding tone.

"You're not the only game in town." It was a woman's voice now. "There's a Saudi sheikh who's ready to pay a half million."

"A half million for two measly fragments when I have almost the whole pot? Don't be ridiculous. I know when you're trying to bluff me. It won't work, kids."

"Well," said another male voice, very casually, "maybe he'll come to you and offer to buy the whole shebang once he has these two pieces."

Liberty pressed her face closer to the grate and caught a glimpse of the room. Roz was out of sight, but in the frame were three faces. One of the men wore a shirt that bore the words SAVE THE BLUE-STRIPED PEPPER FISH. Liberty felt the blood drain from her face. This was unbelievable.

Liberty silently raged. This was Kyumi's fate they were toying with! But her mind suddenly became very clear. She knew exactly what she must do: steal the two pieced-together fragments that Roz already had. The dining room was just around the corner, and the noisy argument below was the perfect camouflage. Liberty slipped across the cool tiles, quieter than a snake slithering through mud. Her concentration was keen. The magnificent fragments seemed to send out an invisible beacon of light, drawing her to them.

Within a quarter of an hour she was back in the bedroom. Tucked underneath her arm was half of the pot that belonged to Kyumi.

We gotta get out of here now. We gotta dress warm, get horses, and get out. She flashed this message in a rapid staccato. *I'll explain later.*

There was an urgency in Liberty's transmission that allowed no room for argument or delay, only action.

Liberty wrapped the large pot fragment, along with some mud, in two pillowcases. The mud, July's brilliant idea, was to insulate the pot against vibrations or any movement that could damage it. Once more Liberty tucked Home Run under her parka.

In the Rancho Eleganza barn they found horses and quickly saddled them up while Liberty explained what she had learned. Roz was the prime customer for black-market Native American artifacts in this area. And if that wasn't a surprise, Liberty's next piece of information certainly was.

The blue-striped-pepper-fish guys? July said increduously. *I can't believe they're the pothunters.*

I recognized two of them.

Liberty described all that she had heard through the vent and how she figured out that the stolen fragments were probably still in the cave near Pink Mesa. And that was where the four twins were heading now. First to Pink Mesa for the two remaining fragments. Liberty was sure that with July's expert tracking skills, they could find the cave and then go on to the hidden kiva.

25.

Night Stalkers and Skinwalkers

A SLICE OF moon hung in an indigo sky. Liberty was reminded of the stories where beyond this nearly black world there was another one of a lighter color that was shining through a crack in the dark dome. They rode together, most often silently, though occasionally the little twins would ask a question about Kyumi, the lost Anasazi girl. Liberty and July had told her story briefly at the beginning of the ride.

"She's like an orphan, a spirit orphan," Molly whimpered. "It's so sad."

"Well, we're going to try and help her."

"Do you think we'll get to meet her?" Charly asked.

"I hope so," July said. "I hope she doesn't give up."

"She won't give up," Liberty said fiercely. After all, she thought, what has she to give up? Kyumi had already lost her life, and her spirit was now doomed to wander a path as endless as the wind.

It was right after they had crossed the rainbow bridge that they sensed trouble. Liberty felt it first, just as she had before—the odd feeling boring into her, right between her shoulder blades.

We're being followed! she flashed.

Then July felt it—a little ping, like a bb grazing his ear. He was prepared. In his tracking book, he had read of an incredible strategy the Navajo had used when eluding an enemy. It was a cloverleaf pattern that involved sending two horses off riderless. He flashed instructions to his sisters.

First they made the huge cloverleaf, each of them splitting off to form one lobe of the leaf. There was a point where each of the two leaves on one side of the stem touched. It was at that point that Charly would climb onto July's horse and Molly onto Liberty's. They would circle behind Blood Mesa near where the holes in the rocks began. July was sure that this would confuse whoever was following them.

Liberty felt Home Run nestle in her collar as she came into the stretch where she expected Molly to appear. *Please let her come, please!* Liberty prayed.

I'm coming, flashed Molly, and within seconds, Liberty saw her younger sister. Molly was crouched over, riding like a jockey. They both reined in their horses as they approached each other. Molly slid over behind Liberty in the saddle. In front of Liberty, strapped to the saddle horn, was the pot, wrapped in the pillowcases packed with mud. She leaned over, gave Molly's horse a whack on its rump, and it galloped off. On the other lobe of the cloverleaf, Charly was just sliding in behind July. So far, so good.

They rode fast through the canyon, bypassing Blood Mesa altogether. The night shimmered, and the twins rode so hard and so fast that tears welled up in their eyes. They rode on through the wind, across the rugged terrain, driven by their vision, drawn by the strange music, pulled by the strong spirit of the oldest girl on earth.

What is that music? Charly asked, for it was becoming stronger and stronger.

You'll find out soon enough, July replied. Oh, he hoped this would work. Where the heck was Liberty? Did she understand the spot where they were to meet?

Then he saw a horse coming.

But wait! It wasn't Liberty. It was just this little bump on the horse, one tiny nubbin—Molly.

What do you mean, "Liberty got off"?

She said she couldn't make it down that steep part with me and the pot. She's going to go on foot the rest of the way. She's way over there. She said that I should get on with you and Charly and we should send this horse off toward some hogback—you'd know where. Then she said that the three of us should go to the cave near Pink Mesa and come back with the stolen fragments and meet her at the hidden kiva.

Did it make sense to split up at all? July was asking himself. He hated it when Liberty changed plans midstream.

But then again, maybe she was right. There was less risk involved to the half of the pot she already carried if she went directly to the kiva and he went to get the other fragments. So the three of them crammed onto July's horse and rode off toward Pink Mesa.

Liberty, meanwhile, scrambled up to a high hole in the rocks above the canyon floor. From here, she commanded a good view, and what she saw flooded her heart with dread, thick and black as mud. An immense figure, dark and shaggy with pointed ears, rose up and howled at the moon. Liberty clutched the precious pot fragment and watched the figure on the ridge with horror. She crouched deeper in the blackness of the hole. She was frightened the way she had been when she was very little and would bury her head under the covers, too scared to look at the antic shadows on her bedroom walls. She was too scared to move, to even breathe. Oh, if only she could be swallowed by this dark mouth in the rock. If only the mouth would shut and sing no more songs and tell no more stories. If only she could slither back into that first world, that world before worlds, in that time before time.

26.

Running Girl

VERA SNOWFLOWER couldn't sleep. She knew why. She was afraid to fall asleep, because the bad dreams might come. But now she felt as if these bad dreams were already here. The owl feathers that she had left in the road the day before seemed to have followed her home. This was the second night she hadn't been able to sleep. Finally she got up and tiptoed out to the clay room. Sometimes when she worked on a pot, it made her feel better, helped her to forget her troubles. She reached for the pot she had been working on for days now, the one with the running figure embedded in its side. No matter how hard she worked on this pot, it was never quite right. And it never would be, Vera realized suddenly. Quickly she picked up a small bone tool and began scraping around the form of the running figure. This figure must run, she thought. This figure was stuck and would always be dragging her feet in the clay. She must be set free. With each quick dig, the figure emerged from its bed of clay, until finally she was no longer part of the pot but was standing free.

More than an hour later, when the blackness of the night was beginning to grow thin, Vera put down her tool. She felt rested, although she had not had a wink of sleep. She felt a strange sense of relief as she looked at her figure of the running girl.

The stars had begun to fade, and Liberty did not know how many hours had passed. She had cramps in her legs now, and a trickle of blood ran down her chin from where she had bitten her lip in fear. How long could she stay locked in this position? July and Molly and Charly might be waiting for her, or worse yet, might have already been caught by the skinwalker. There was an urgency growing in her. Something was pushing her, pushing her out of the dark mouth in the canyon wall. She knew the dawn was coming. It was now or never. She felt Home Run in her parka. He was right near her heart, which was beating faster. Did he feel it? He must. She watched the sky. There wasn't much time, but she couldn't run well carrying the pot in her arms. She would have to strap the bundle to her back. She took off her belt and her sweater and improvised a sling backpack. It felt good, more secure than carrying the pot in her arms. She crept to the rim of the hole. There was no sign of the skinwalker or anyone else. It was perhaps two or three miles still to Blood Mesa. The sky was growing lighter by the second.

Somewhere on the other side of that horizon, the sun was drinking up the night. Liberty rose and broke out of the dark hole. She scrambled down the embankment and sprang toward the lightening horizon. Little cyclones of desert dust exploded around her feet. To someone who didn't know better, she might have looked like that ancient humpbacked flute player finally released from his rock. Liberty Starbuck herself felt something break loose within her, something that was not quite courage and not quite will, something that had been living within her always and now had surfaced without warning. Liberty ran with all her heart and with all her might and with all her soul. She ran for the dawn.

Liberty broke Blood Mesa before the sun slipped over the horizon. She arrived at the kiva, and Kyumi, shimmering and white in her buckskin, stood before her.

They aren't here—July and my little sisters?

> *No, no. Not yet.* Kyumi was enthralled with the
> immense fragment that Liberty had brought her.
> *It is a mystery how one part of a pot can break into
> such tiny pieces and then another like these can
> remain so big. They were not carried far by the river.
> They must have fallen into a nice sandy, muddy
> bank. And then, after hundreds of years, after the
> river changed its course and dried, were found. You
> were smart to pack it in mud.*

It was my brother's idea.

Liberty felt she should give credit where credit was due. With each passing second, she was becoming more agitated. Where could those kids be? Could the skinwalker have caught them?

"Well, what can I tell you?" July said to the man with the beard. "They dawdle. It's part of being six years old. Weren't you ever six?"

"Would you just watch your mouth, kid!" the man snarled. While July caused a distraction, the little twins dawdled and dropped a trail of press-on nails as an unmistakable sign of their presence.

"You should see how long it takes them to get dressed for school in the morning. You know, by the time they play with their Toilet Roll Kingdom and all that, it's at least twenty minutes between getting each sock on."

"What's the Toilet Roll Kingdom?" the blond girl with the Indian-style braids and headband asked.

"Would you shut up, River Fire."

"What a stupid name," mumbled Charly.

"What did you say?" The girl spoke harshly.

"I said what a stupid name," Charly repeated clearly.

"Well, you are a real little capitalist piggy of a child."

"What's that?" Molly asked.

"It means you're spoiled rotten, think you deserve it all, disgustingly materialistic."

"Well, what do you call yourselves?" July asked. "You're failed capitalists—you just steal from Native Americans and sell to rich slobs like Roz."

"It rhymes," Molly said gleefully. "Rich slobs like Roz . . . Rich slobs like Roz." She started dancing around in the dark and dropping fingernails. Luckily they had brought a good supply. After all, they had thought they would be spending their time at a beauty spa.

There was a sharp crack, then a wail. "He hit me! He hit me!" Molly screamed. July was at the guy's throat in a second.

"You hit my sister again and that's it." But they were stronger than July and pulled him off the man with the beard, the one they called David Skyhawk and to whom Molly had already endeared herself by calling him David Poop Hawk.

July was livid. "Just kill us right here. Then we'll never show you where this place is. You'll never see the greatest discovery in North American archaeology."

"He's right, he's right," said another heavyset fellow. "Just cool it, David. A deal's a deal—at least in this case it better be."

It was July who had forged the deal. They had indeed discovered the cave, and the two stolen fragments plus many others. The people who had caught them there, the "environmentalists," were no more interested in the blue-striped pepper fish than they were in the man in the moon. The real reason they did not want the river diverted was that it would bring many people and too much farmland close to their places of trade—their happy pot-hunting grounds— their stashes of some of the greatest Anasazi finds of recent years, which fueled their thriving black-market business. Now July had promised to lead the four ringleaders to a virtual gold mine. There was just one condition. They must let him take the two fragments with him. Once they were all at the cliff dwelling, July promised, there would be many more shards, much more valuable than the two. All he wanted was these two fragments. Those would buy his and his sisters' silence and would in turn give the pothunters the keys to a hidden cliff city chock-full of unbelievable treasures. What the pothunters had not bargained for were these three smart-alecky mouths and all the yapping and dawdling, but of course that was part of July's plan. He was hoping to lay a trail so someone would find them before they reached Blood Mesa. Once they got there, there would be the problem of trying to get those big slobs inside. So that might buy them a little more time.

But he should have known: The heavyset guy, the one they called Joe—the only one who didn't have some dumb made-up Indian name—was actually called Dynamite Joe.

"Oh, this guy is to dynamite what diamond cutters are to the jewelry trade," David Skyhawk said.

"This isn't going to take much at all," Dynamite Joe was saying as he examined the crevice. "I just want everyone to stand back. You say there's a corridor, kid, that runs for about fifty feet?"

"Yes," July said nervously.

"Well, I'll tell you what." Dynamite Joe's fleshy face lit up. There was an ugly gleam in his eye, and his thick lips split into a smile that revealed big yellow teeth. "This is going to be like a race. You little guys squeeze right in there and see how fast you can run. I'm putting this on a fifteen-second fuse. So that's fifteen seconds for you to get out of range."

"I thought we had a deal!" July screamed. "We promised silence and we'd show you the place."

"Well, think of this"—Joe held up a stick of dynamite—"as our little insurance policy, just in case one of the little dawdlers starts talking." And with that, Dynamite Joe picked up Charly and Molly. They screamed as he began stuffing them through the opening in the rock. July had no choice. He leaped to the crevice and slid in after his little sisters.

27.

On the Flint-Knappers' Terrace

LIBERTY THOUGHT she heard a scream; then there was an explosion. The noise rumbled through the rock rooms of the cliff dwelling. The bones of the skeletons trembled. Little bits of dirt fell from the walls and the ceiling. The next thing she knew, July and Charly and Molly were standing before her in the kiva.

Quickly! Kyumi spoke. *Follow me.*

Is that her? She looks like a . . . a flickering candle, flashed Molly.

A kind of flame . . . , Charly added. The little twins could not stop looking at her. They were drawn to her like moths to a light.

Come quickly—leave the fragments there, July.

July laid the two stolen fragments down by the other shards and the big piece Liberty had brought. As he laid down the last piece, all the pieces began to radiate slivers of light. The earth beneath them turned pale gold, and suddenly there was a shimmering glow. July and Liberty blinked as the pot became whole before their very eyes.

Come! Now! Kyumi ordered. The voices of River Fire, David Skyhawk, Dynamite Joe, and a fourth man called White Buffalo were very close. July and Liberty knew exactly what Kyumi was doing. She was leading them away from the kiva. The kiva, which had been defiled by greed once, must not be defiled again.

But greed had filled the dwelling like a noxious gas. Still, they must lead these pothunters away from the pot, away from the bones. "This way," July called out, loud and clear. Left, right, left again; up a ladder, across one terrace, then to another. Finally they arrived on the flint-knappers' terrace. The impact of Dynamite Joe's blast had dislodged one of the boulders of the terrace, and now they seemed to be standing on the edge of the world. It was a sheer five-hundred-foot drop to the canyon floor below. Low pink clouds lay in streaks on the dawn horizon. The mountains were a deep lavender, and the sky was clear, not yet blue. The new day was breaking. Liberty, caught in its amazing beauty, felt as if they were on the brink of a sixth world. They were indeed like the Air Spirits, ready to climb through the dome of the morning sky.

"Okay, you little creeps, the game is up!"

Now none of the Starbuck twins was afraid. They were mad, fiercely mad. Anger jangled in the channels. They remembered the myths their mother had read to them. They remembered the tales that described the journey of the people from one world into the next, where every person, animal, and insect was expected to bring something—a skill, some knowledge, or seed like brother Turkey, strong silk like Spider Woman, or even good magic—but something! And what stood before them were the greediest people on earth—these were the dream snatchers. Suddenly July felt a shape in his hand. Had it been Kyumi? Had she placed the ancient sling in his hand? Molly and Charly each felt a small, perfectly round stone in her palm, and what was it that Home Run had uncovered? An old stone ax? They were being mysteriously, magically armed. Dynamite Joe lunged toward Liberty. But July was fast, and he used the sling well. River Fire screamed as blood and yellow teeth burst from Dynamite Joe's mouth. Joe staggered backward, and then he simply disappeared over the edge of the terrace.

The children raised their stones, their slings, the ax, as River Fire, David Skyhawk, and White Buffalo cowered at the edge of the flint-knappers' terrace. They could not see Kyumi, but they felt they were being held by an invisible power. The twins felt the power, too. It was as if all the old flint knappers had come to stand with the Starbuck children. Indeed, all the people of the ancient settlement were beside them, backing them up, confronting the greed that huddled at the edge of the terrace.

"They're here! Oh, my word! Oh, thank heavens." Aunt Honey, followed by Putt and Zanny and three Navajo tribal policemen, burst onto the terrace.

I have never in my life seen Aunt Honey without eye makeup, Liberty flashed.

When she gets finished hugging us, we'll be able to see, too, Molly replied.

This must be like being hugged by a boa constrictor, Charly added.

"Oh, my lord!" Aunt Honey was blubbering. "When Zanny came in and told me all four of you were missing, and then when Roz accused you children of stealing her precious museum-quality pot pieces, not even caring what happened to you kids, it was all too much." Honey began to sob again. "Then she actually tried to prevent Zanny from calling Putt. But, oh, that left hook of yours, Zanny!"

"Left hook!" all four Starbuck children blurted.

"I know. I never knew I had it in me," Zanny said in a dazed tone.

"You mean you hit Roz?"

"Knocked her flat," Honey said.

"Got her right in the chops," Putt added.

"Nothing that an herbal wrap won't be able to fix up," Zanny added with a smile. Liberty instantly forgave her for the mud baths. Zanny was no sellout, and neither was Aunt Honey.

Another policeman arrived on the terrace. "There's a fat guy stuck on a ledge about twenty feet down below this terrace. Looks like he's wedged pretty tight between a couple of rocks."

In all of the commotion, the twins had not even noticed Vera SnowFlower.

"Vera!" Liberty exclaimed when she finally saw her.

"Vera was really the one to lead us here. She found the press-on nails that you must have dropped, and then very quickly we began to pick up the trail," Putnam said.

Vera was standing, transfixed, staring at the spot where Kyumi had shimmered just minutes before. Could she see Kyumi? Liberty wondered. Could she somehow feel her spirit? But where had Kyumi gone?

28.

A Last Visit

"I CAN'T BELIEVE that we'll never see her again. I just can't believe it." Liberty sighed. All four twins stood now on the roof of their house on the mesa. It was time for bed, but Madeline had let the twins go up to watch the stars after she read to them. She had flown out to New Mexico the moment she had heard the incredible news about the harrowing narrow escape her four children had experienced. The children were all fine, but Aunt Honey, they feared, would never recover. Even now they heard her sobbing downstairs.

"I'll never forgive myself, Madeline. I just won't. I'll never recover from this and that horrible Roz. I can't believe it. Her greed, her monumental greed! She has had everything all her life. Why did she need more things that weren't even hers?"

"Now, Honey," Madeline soothed, "it was not your fault."

"None of this was your fault." The children heard Putnam's voice. "You thought you were doing me a favor, after all."

A favor! The word flashed among all the twins.

"Oh, those horrible, horrible people," the twins heard Zanny exclaim. "And to think they tried to pass themselves off as environmentalists, friends of the blue-striped pepper fish."

As the grown-ups talked, things became clearer to Liberty and July. And the clearer they became, the more keenly the twins felt the danger to which they had been exposed, and realized how awful those people were.

July, Liberty flashed. *They put the bone bead in Marguerite Greyeyes's drawer and in our jelly-bean box. I'm sure of it. Remember when we came into the trading post when we first found the fragments that day? There were two of them sitting under the cottonwood tree, and we were yakking away about the fragments as we came up the path.*

The scene came back to July. Liberty was right. The little twins had been arguing about who would carry the fragments. *And that wolf, that skinwalker on the ridge. He was one, too. They really are terrorists,* July added.

It was as if a cold wind had blown through the channels.

"With friends like that, who needs enemies?" Madeline sighed. "I'd better make sure those kids get to bed. They have half a dozen interviews tomorrow, and then on Thursday, Dr. Ridley would like them to all come down to the university and address his archaeology class."

I wonder if she'll let us wear our press-on nails? Molly flashed.

Oooh, yeah. And maybe our satin tuxedos and the top hats, added Charly.

You guys, this isn't an ice show. It's a college archaeology course, July flashed.

They knew they would have to go back sometime before all the archaeologists came with their shovels, their picks, and their screens and began marking off the hidden dwelling into grids for measuring and digging. The archaeologists would see the bones and the pot, but Dr. Ridley was a good soul and knew to respect the bones of the first people of this country. It would all be done according to their customs and their wishes. Everything would be restored to the Anasazi—to their own museums and their own archives.

The children had wanted to see the cliff dwelling once more before they were to guide Dr. Ridley and his team through, but they had not expected Vera SnowFlower to come tapping on their skylight two nights after their adventure. At first Liberty thought the noise was the vines scratching on the glass again, but then she saw the moonlit face looking down through the skylight.

"We must go now!" Vera said. "Please take me!" There was no way they could refuse. So the four Starbucks saddled up their ponies once more. Vera rode behind Liberty. The moon, a mere slice three nights before, had ripened into a perfect silver melon as it cast a trail of light toward Blood Mesa.

"It's gone!" Liberty blurted as they entered the kiva. "Somebody has stolen it. The pot is gone."

"It can't be," July gasped.

"No, no," Vera said. "I feel it, I feel it here." But how could she know? She had never even seen it. "Look," Vera said. "Was it there, next to the bones?"

"Yes," Liberty and July replied.

"See, there is a circle of cornmeal sprinkled on the ground. That is a sign. And the prayer bundle is just there." She pointed toward a deerskin bundle with a cluster of dried plants, a painted stick, and some feathers sticking out from inside it. "This is good. This is the way to send a spirit to the spirit land."

"But the pot?" Liberty and July both asked.

"It is here," Vera replied firmly.

And then there was a soft glow in front of them. Kyumi appeared, dazzling in her beauty. In her arms she held what appeared to be the pot—seamless and gleaming. And yet not exactly the pot.

It looks like a hologram, July flashed.

> *It is the pot, July. It is in the form that I shall take with me now. It is whole—whole in spirit for eternity, since all the fragments have at last been found. I don't need the actual pieces for where I am*

*going. Just as I do not need my earthly body. But I
am here.* The voice, as always, was in the channels.
And before the twins could ask the question, she
answered it. *Yes, Vera SnowFlower can hear me,
for she is my kin. She is the master potter of this
generation.*

All four Starbuck twins turned and looked at Vera. She
stood so still, it was as if she were not even breathing, but
her eyes were brimming.

> *She is the new vessel, the vessel for a new life. She
> is the master potter for the spirit of my clay. Now
> follow me, for this is my last night of being a restless
> spirit. This is the last night of my spirit's long, long
> journey. It usually takes four days to make this
> journey, but for me it has taken nearly six hundred
> years. Now I am ready—*

But your moccasins, Molly said as they climbed to the
flint-knappers' terrace. *You're wearing them backward.*

> *Oh,* laughed Kyumi, and once more the sound of
> her laughter was like chimes in the wind. *That is
> so bad ghosts cannot follow me to the land of the
> spirits, to the land where I will meet my mother,
> my father, my grandfather, and my baby sister.*

Then she came very close to each one of them. First to Vera: *My kin,* she whispered. Then to Charly and Molly: *My brave ones.* They felt her light. And finally to July and Liberty: *My hero twins!* The voice trembled in the channels. They could see her eyes looking deep into their own, and through them, they could see the stars still twinkling over the canyon.

And then she left. The children watched as a wisp of pale light swirled from the edge of the terrace, out across the canyon. And the light that was Kyumi streaked across the sky and faded into the desert night.